Potent

TB Wittkofsky

Kelsey Anne Lovelady

Contents

Author's Note

Dear Reader,

As authors, we wanted to take a moment to discuss the use of the pronoun set "fae/faer" and shed light on its correct usage and importance in promoting inclusivity.

In recent years, there has been a growing recognition and understanding of gender diversity. People identify themselves along a spectrum beyond the binary categories of male and female. To respect and honor this diversity, it is crucial that we embrace inclusive language and provide individuals with pronouns that affirm their gender identity.

The pronoun set "fae/faer" is an example of a gender-neutral neo-pronouns that some individuals may use to express their non-binary or genderqueer identity. Fae (pronounced like "fey") is a subject pronoun, similar to "he" or "she," while faer (pronounced like "fair") is an object pronoun, similar to "him" or "her." It's important to note that these pronouns are just one of many sets that people may use, and different individuals may have different preferences.

Using the correct pronouns is a matter of respect and recognition. When we use someone's preferred pronouns, we validate their identity and create a safer, more inclusive environment. It shows that we see and acknowledge them for who they are, and that their gender identity is valid and valued.

As authors, we strive to create narratives that reflect the diverse experiences and identities of our readers. We believe that storytelling has the power to inspire empathy and understanding, fostering a society where everyone's voice is heard and valued. By incorporating inclusive language, such as using pronoun sets like fae/faer for Puck a.k.a. Robin Goodfellow, we hope to contribute to this ongoing progress.

Warm regards,
TB Wittkofsky and Kelsey Anne Lovelady

1

Oberon

I sat hunched over my desk, scribbling away mindlessly on a notepad. Between doodles of my once powerful kingdom, I was making notes on the financial sheets for my new business. I had been one of the most powerful beings in the universe, but now I was barely known by anyone. A tech mogul named Obe was all I amounted to now. Sure, for a mortal that would be a happy life, to be a millionaire playboy, but not for me.

The ones that believed in me were locked away in the psych ward. Faerie weren't real, not to the human mind anyway. The ones who supported my alter ego had no idea who I truly was, and honestly, I wasn't sure they'd care. As long as they could keep their fortune and fame, they'd go along with anything and everything.

The world had changed a lot over the last hundred years for a Faerie King like me. If it isn't clear by now, my name is Oberon. *The* Oberon that served as the inspiration behind William Shakespeare's *Midsummer Night's Dream*. The one that's best known for turning a man into an ass in a jealous fit of rage. Truth be told, it was Will himself that I had actually turned into an ass.

Titania and I parted ways for the last time over a hundred years ago. She left me to be with a mortal, as she did often. But this last time, she left for good. In her defense, months went by before I noticed she was gone. I was an asshole towards her, and she rightfully left me. Time after time she would leave me and I would say all the right things to win her back, but not this time.

Nothing I could say this time would change her mind. She wanted to live a mortal life, and there was nothing I could do about it. As the years dragged by, I dragged myself away from my kingdom. I decided to live a mortal life like Titania. My hope was that it would keep my mind off of her. I would go out and live the bachelor life like the mortal men did when they had small dicks and lots of money.

"You even failed at that, Oberon."

The voices in my head grew louder once I left my kingdom. They were the voices that once caused me to kill men for no reason other than pure ecstasy. Being an immortal being doesn't mean that I was immune to the same mental disorders as the mortals. In my kingdom, it wasn't nearly as bad, though.

"You belong to us out here. This is our kingdom."

I sighed and stood from my desk as I shook my head to clear my thoughts. Pushing my round, wireframe glasses up my nose, I took in a deep breath and listened to the beat of the techno music blaring around me. I closed my eyes and embraced the vibrations of the beat flowing through my body.

"Never good enough."

"Failure."

"You're no King."

"Coward."

"That's why she left you."

"You didn't deserve her, Oberon."

"Oberon..."

"Oberon..."

"Enough!" I shouted and threw a jolt of energy at the face of the radio. The red ball of pure power pushed past the frame and sparks blew out of the radio. Both the music and the voices died down simultaneously.

"Oberon," I heard a voice come from behind me.

I ran a hand across my raven black hair and pushed it away from the shaved side of my head. "Puck," I finally said before turning around to face faer. "What do you need?"

"First, to make sure you're okay," Puck replied with a hint of concern in faer voice. "I was calling your name, and you just sat there tapping your foot with your eyes closed."

"The voices, Puck," I explained as I rubbed my temples and shut my eyes again. "They're getting louder every day."

Puck lifted my chin up with faer finger. I opened my eyes and saw Puck staring deep into my soul. "My King, we will not let them win. We'll figure out a way to quiet them down."

"Not for as long as you're on the mortal plane."

My nostrils flared as I clenched my jaw. I brushed faer hand away and turned around to walk to the window of my penthouse apartment. Puck's footsteps got closer until fae stood beside me, placing a hand across my back and around my shoulder.

I looked down and over at Puck. Fae had been my most loyal friend for my entire life. The only one from my court I had brought with me when I left my kingdom behind. Faer short, disheveled, bleach blonde hair rested against my shoulder and I smiled.

"Puck?"

"Yes, my King?"

Pausing for a moment, I took a deep breath. I closed my eyes and squeezed them tight before I could speak again. "Is she coming back?" I finally asked.

Puck's breath hitched as I asked the question. I knew the answer to the questions better than fae did, but it wouldn't stop me from asking. I had hoped that Puck would tell me one day that yes, she would come back.

"She'll never come back to you."

"She's successful."

"You're a failure."

"Failure."

My breath quickened as I fought the sound of the voices filling my mind. I felt faer hand squeeze my shoulder. It wasn't a squeeze intended to hurt, but instead one meant to comfort, to remind me that Puck was there with me.

I knew that. I knew I had Puck and I always would have fae. That wasn't who I wanted, though. It wasn't who I needed at the moment. And it wasn't Puck's fault. It wasn't anyone's fault but mine that Titania was gone and never coming back.

"She always does," Puck finally answered, faer eyes clenched shut.

I shook my head. "Not this time," I argued. "Why would she?"

Puck took faer arm back from around me and slid in front of me, laying faer chin against my chest. " 'Why would she?' " Fae asked, looking up at me. "Because you're Oberon. You're the Orpheus to her Eurydice, the Osiris to her Isis, the Mark Antony to her Cleopatra, the King to her Queen, my lord."

"You're something to her alright."

"The failure to her success."

"The ex to her life."

I shook my head, looking away from Puck and at the radio face I had blown apart mere minutes before. I balled up my fist and slammed my eyes shut as the voices rang in my head louder and louder.

"Shut the *fuck* up!" I shouted, my eyes shooting open and glowing black. Puck stumbled backwards and fell over the back of the red leather couch framing my living area.

I could feel the way my chest heaved, trying to keep up with the rapid pounding of my heart within. My breath came in ragged pants, like a dog starved for water. "Leave, Puck," I commanded in a more calm and measured tone than the one I had just shouted in.

"My lord..." Puck started.

"Puck, I said leave. Get the *fuck* out," I ordered fae.

Puck lowered faer head and rolled off the couch. Fae walked to the door, stopping only to look back at me in all my drowning misery and self loathing. I saw fae bite faer lip and blink away what I could only imagine was a tear before fae turned and left my penthouse.

I walked to the very couch Puck had stumbled over and laid down. Turning on the television, I closed my eyes and let my mind wander as the television played in the background.

"Titania," I called out as I walked through the eerily quiet halls of my palace. "Where have you gone, woman?" I whispered and stroked my chin.

I continued wandering aimlessly through the corridors looking for my Queen. Not finding her, I wandered back to the throne room to see if anybody in there knew where she was. I hoped that Puck would be in there and could help me track her down.

When was the last time I saw her? It was a good question, and one I couldn't really answer. As bad as it sounded, being a king took a lot of time. I was gone for days at a time handling both internal and external affairs.

Surely it couldn't have been more than a week. Or could it have been? It wasn't more than a month, for sure. Or was it?

I shook my head and pushed open the door to the throne room. The normally bright and beaming throne room was draped in darkness, drastically deepening the fear I held within me. Worst of all, when I got close enough to see the throne, I could make out a faceless figure sitting on *my* throne.

"What're you doing?" I called out, pointing at the scoundrel in my seat. "That throne is reserved for the King. Me."

"I'm the King in this plane, Oberon."

I looked around for the source of the voice that seemed to come from everywhere but in front of me. "This is my kingdom!" Stomping my foot, I took a step forward.

A step was all I could take before my entire body froze. I felt my muscles constrict and my throat collapse. My nostrils flared, trying desperately for air. There was a numbness shrouding my shell.

"You are my kingdom, Obe."

I attempted to refute, but my lips felt like they were sewed shut. Every time I tried to separate my lips, I felt a pull on them keeping them from opening. My nostrils flared again as my eyes stayed on the faceless figure.

"You're a failure. At everything you do. Including running this kingdom."

My heart beat heavily against my chest, a dull thud sounding one after another. I willed myself forward, just barely moving my left leg forward. The seizing feeling of my muscles tightened to an almost unbearable pain level.

"You're a failure at being a King to all of these people. Look at how the world is falling apart."

I clenched my fist. It was the only movement I felt like I had control of. I opened them and took a deep breath.

"Look at how you drove her away. Your insolence caused her to leave. The crumbling of your kingdom came soon after, but you were too self-consumed to see it."

"Shut up!" I yelled, shooting up from my slumber. I panted heavily and looked around me at the empty room. The only sound was that of the television playing some tabloid channel.

Suddenly, a boudoir picture of a woman with a pink pixie cut flashed on the screen as the report switched to paparazzi chasing her down. I stood and turned up the tv with a snap of my fingers.

"Tati Hastings has been spotted going to Russo's on Main Street. She appears to be meeting with Casting Director Steven Sheehan to discuss a role in his upcoming, unannounced, untitled film," the tv reported.

My eyes grew wide. I dialed Puck's number and waited for faer to answer. When fae finally did, I shouted, "meet me at Russo's now!"

"Tati Hastings was just named the best plus-sized actress in the country. The cover, showing Hastings in a boudoir photo-shoot style, has claimed to be left as is by People Magazine. A spokesperson has confirmed that this photo has not been airbrushed or photoshopped," droned the voice on the television.

"Must they *always* qualify their statements with 'plus-sized'?" I sighed.

Unphased by my exasperated slumping, Lark followed my head with the flat iron they were using to curl my hair. "You know those skinny bitches are threatened by you. They have to find something to minimize your work and accomplishments."

I looked back at the newscaster, who was airing the story about me. "She really is a skinny bitch."

"And that's why she's on divorce number three," Dragonfly mumbled as he brushed blush onto my cheeks.

The rest of my court and glam team hesitated to laugh until I did. "Like she can afford a third round of alimony." My catty comment sent another wave of laughter through my kitchen. It felt good to hear the support and adoration of me bounce off of the granite countertops and white walls.

It really was good to be the Queen.

I may have technically relinquished my title when I left my ex-husband and the Faerie Kingdom behind, but I still had my court and my power. The glamor I needed to live was easily won once I came to Hollywood. While I was no longer Titania, Queen of Faeries, I was Tati Hastings, Queen of L.A. I ran this town. Hell, I practically built the city.

"What are we thinking for rings today?" Fern asked as she put the top coat on my nails.

"Oh, you know I have so many to choose from. Bring me the box." Fern nodded and immediately fetched the ring box where I kept all of my prizes and mementos from loves long gone.

My family was convinced they were all family heirlooms or lucky finds on my part, but they were in fact all the wedding and engagement rings I'd collected in the last century or so. I was more fond of some than others—I'd choose the 1960s Jackie O look-alike from Joseph over the 1920s Art Deco Jack Wier and Sons from Edgar any day. "The 1958 Van Cleef & Arpels Sens," I said. A unique ring with baguette-cut diamonds and a pear-cut ruby. This gift from Hugh had always been my good luck charm, and I needed all the luck I could get that day.

The land line phone rang loudly, but only for a second before I waved my hand through the air. The receiver floated off the wall and rested itself next to my right ear. Normally I would have used my hands, but my nails were still drying, and I wasn't about to undo Fern's gorgeous work. "Hastings Residence," I greeted, slipping into my American dialect.

"Good morning, Ms. Hastings."

"Good morning, Jonathan!" It was the handsome young man who acted as the gate guard for the neighborhood. I may have been spoken for, but I was still thankful that our gated community hired college students looking for easy part-time jobs to be security. It certainly kept things interesting.

"Your bodyguard has returned with your children."

"Marvelous. Send them in."

"Right away, Ms. Hastings."

Once Jonathan hung up, I floated the phone back to its place on the wall. A quick scan of the kitchen and living room confirmed that nothing inhuman had been left out or made obvious. "Fern?" I called.

"On it." The petite sprite flew through the three-story home, looking for anything that gave away our immortal origins. It took her less than a minute to come back. "Charade maintained, my Queen."

"Good." I loved my children far too much to expose them to the dramatic and complex world of faeries. And if the rest of the mortal world ever found out about my true origins? Everything I worked for would crumble before my very eyes. I couldn't put my family through that. They were going through enough as it was.

Less than a minute later, the front door opened to reveal Bear escorting my daughters from the car into our home. Bear lived up to his name□. At over six-and-a-half feet tall, no one would ever expect him to be a faerie. Most simply chalked his intimidating figure to being a gym addict who might dabble in performance-enhancing drugs. He truly was the perfect specimen to protect my family. Especially my children.

"We're home!" The unadulterated joy and youth in the voice was a dead giveaway for Samira. At only seven years old, the world was still full of wonder, and she hadn't quite gotten to the age of disliking school yet. Primarily because she was too likable to be the target of any bullying. Many had tried, all had been disarmed by her natural charm. Of course, the lack of homework was also a wonderful perk.

My glam team stepped away from me, anticipating Sami to come running in for a hug as she always did. Thankfully, my nails were dry enough to get the use of my hands back. "There's my little one!" I greeted, scooping the child up into my arms and setting her in my lap.

Malika was the next to enter. While the excitement of school had worn off for her, the smile on her face indicated she was still just as popular as she had been yesterday. And why wouldn't she be? She was beautiful, likable, and partook in extracurricular activities. "Guess who's up for Prom Queen!" She called excitedly, striking a dramatic pose with her arms open wide.

The proclamation drew applause from myself and my entire glam team. Even Sami clapped, despite not completely knowing or understanding the exciting honor the title of Prom Queen was.

Amira, Malika's twin, was the last child to enter. Those twins could not be more diametrically opposed. Where Malika was already on her way to becoming one of the most successful influencers and beauty gurus on the internet, Amira's focus was exclusively on her studies. But that didn't mean that she was easily overshadowed. She slammed three open letters down onto the granite top bar. "Columbia, Harvard, and Princeton all said yes!"

It shouldn't have come as a surprise to anyone; Amira had always been studious and got the best grades in her class consistently. Amira earned her way into those schools. And she didn't have to pretend to be on the crew team to do it.

Another round of applause spread through the kitchen. I truly was the happiest mother on the planet. *Maybe I should adopt more. Sami will be awfully lonely when Amira goes to college and Malika starts building her makeup empire. And obviously, children thrive under my parenting. Something to talk to Chad about once Bradley gets his shit together and signs the divorce papers.*

I kissed Sami's cheek, saying, "I am so proud of you, my girls."

"Thanks, Mama!" Sami threw her arms around my neck, hugging and kissing me before sliding off of my lap and running up to her room to put her backpack away.

"Thanks Mom," my twins replied in unison, kissing my cheeks and following the example of their younger sister.

"Oh, Malika, there are a bunch of packages that came for you. They looked like they were PR packages, so I put them in your makeup room."

Malika sighed. "No rest for the weary," she mumbled.

"You're very lucky, my dear. Not everyone gets to do what they love as their jobs," I lectured.

Malika rolled her eyes as she smiled. "I know, mom." With another kiss on the cheek, my twins disappeared upstairs; Amira went to the library to study, and Malika to her beauty room to film makeup reviews.

With loving sighs, I and my glam team returned to the task at hand, preparing me for the most important meeting of my career. "How are they doing? With everything?" Lark asked.

"I do my best to shield them, but Bradley certainly doesn't make it easy with his petty behavior."

Bear cracked his knuckles. "Should I teach him how to be a mature father?"

"Thank you, Bear darling, but the last thing I need is for him to accuse me of putting a hit out on him... But if you happen to see him walking at any crosswalk in the city, I suppose all I can ask is that you drive fast enough to make it impossible to read the license plate."

My court laughed at my dark joke, though I could tell there were a few who were wondering if I was serious or not. It wouldn't have mattered either way. Just curiosity on their parts.

A little while later, the landline rang again, indicating another visitor to the neighborhood. This time, I walked to the phone and picked it up with my hand. I couldn't risk my children seeing anything that would be too difficult to explain with mortal logic. "Hello?"

"Sorry to bug you again, Ms. Hastings, but Mr. Bradshaw is here to see you."

I beamed upon hearing the name. "Send him in," I ordered before hanging up.

"Now, don't you go messing up your makeup! This is very good liquid lipstick," Dragonfly warned.

"I make no promises," I told him with a wink.

The glam team started cleaning their workspaces and gathering their supplies the mortal way—they knew better than to risk using their powers with my daughters in the house and my fiancé on the way. I could tell that they weren't fans of doing things the difficult way. I was still their Queen, and they were going to do everything I asked of them without question or complaint. That obedience mostly came from their respect for me as opposed to their fear of me.

I couldn't lie, it was good to have respect based on affection rather than fear. Machiavelli might have thought that it was better to be feared than loved, but that's probably because he was a man that only a mother could love. And even she barely tolerated the man rather than loving him.

Yes, it was far better to be loved. Especially when I was loved by my court, my girls, the love of my immortal life, and practically the entire world.

It was a very different experience than my marriage with Bradley. Or even... him.

The front door opened before the intrusive thoughts of the past could overwhelm me, and my darling fiancée entered with two handfuls of grocery bags. It certainly paid to have a hobbyist cook for a fiancée on those nights that I couldn't cook for the children myself.

"Hello!" Chad called to the house. I was the first to the door, taking the bags from his hands. I pressed my body to his and pushed myself onto my toes, puckering my lips. "Mm, hello, gorgeous." Chad read my behavior well and gave me a quick kiss on the lips. His black beard tickled my chin and cheeks, making me giggle.

"Lipstick!" Dragonfly called from the kitchen.

Chad and I broke our kiss quickly with laughter and eye-rolling. "Is this everything?" I asked.

"Yep. Keeping it really simple tonight."

"Thank you so much for doing this, darling."

"Of course! Anything I can do to help my girl and her girls." Gods, he was so thoughtful. So caring. I really hit the jackpot with him.

About damn time. Pretty sure I've had way too much drama for the last 1500 years, I thought.

We brought the bags into the kitchen and put everything away. Chad asked, "Are the girls home?"

"They beat you by a full five minutes. Malika has some makeup to review for her channel, so just be careful about disturbing her. Amira is studying as usual. Make sure she eats—you know how she forgets meals when she's reading."

"And Sami?"

"Here I am!" Right on cue, my seven-year-old daughter came running down the stairs. She threw herself into Chad's arms. He hugged her tight. Anyone who didn't know better would think that he was her legal adoptive father rather than Bradley.

"There's my girl! How was school today?"

"It was okay. But I could use some help with my math homework."

Chad puffed up with pride. "Well, you've come to the right place, little lady. You know I won an award for math when I was just a little older than you."

"You'll help me?" Sami asked excitedly.

"Of course, kiddo." Chad's reassurance to my daughter was punctuated by my placing his straw fedora on her head. It completely covered her tight curls and fell over her eyes, but Sami always loved the hats my fiancée wore. All we could see were her pearly teeth that would never have to see braces a day in her life.

"Thanks Chad! When can we start?"

"How about after dinner, kiddo? I hear you just got home with your sisters. You all deserve a break."

"Cool!" And with that, Sami went running off back to her room.

Chad and I laughed as we watched her go. "She really likes you," I mused to him.

"At least one of them does."

I sighed. "Give the twins some time. The divorce has been hard on them and he's doing everything to make it even harder than it already is."

"I know," Chad replied. I looked into his sweet face and could see the sadness in his eyes.

Before I could provide any form of comfort, Fern interrupted us. "Ms. Hastings. If we don't leave now, we're going to be late."

"Go on. I'll be okay," Chad encouraged, seeing the inner argument spill onto my face.

"You're sure?"

"I promise. Go be brilliant and get the part."

I grinned up at him. "Don't I always?"

Chad chuckled and placed a sweet kiss on my lips again.

"Lipstick!" Was all he needed to be told to not make the kiss too long and too messy.

"I'll see you soon," I assured him as I grabbed my purse.

3
Oberon

I sat in the car with Puck in the driver's seat. I took a deep breath and looked at faer. "Puck, are we sure this is the right thing to do?" I ran a hand through my hair and pushed it to the other side of my head.

"Are *we* sure?" Puck scoffed. "I told you this was a bad idea. You need to leave her be, Oberon."

"You're right," I sighed. "I must do this."

"That's not-" Puck started before I opened the door of the car and strolled to the restaurant entrance. I took a deep breath and opened it. When I walked into the restaurant, the transition lenses on my glasses faded from black to clear.

I glanced around the room, scanning it for Titania. I could hear chatter throughout the room as people whispered.

"Is that Obe?"

"He's been a recluse for years."

"I can't believe he's out in public at this time of day."

I smirked as I continued my scan of the room before I finally spotted her. Her beautiful curves were like waves of the ocean calming me just by being in her presence. Her pink pixie cut shimmered like the faerie she was and drew me in. She was my Queen.

At her table, I spotted two men and one other woman. Titania was laughing as she talked, causing the table to fall in love with her with every word she spoke. She had that effect on people, especially on me.

"You're going to screw this up."

"You don't know that. She loves me."

"Loved you, not loves."

"You don't know that."

"She's not with you, is she?"

"Quiet," I shushed myself and the voices in my mind.

I put my head down and hurried to the bathroom, making sure to walk close to Titania's table. Once I was behind her chair, I gently bumped the back of her chair with my hip. She was holding a glass of wine that spilled all over the front of her blouse.

I almost felt bad. Almost.

I continued my trek to the bathroom before sliding through the door and hopping on the counter. Puck appeared beside me, crouched on top of the sink, waiting.

"That was it? A butt bump?" Puck asked.

"I had to get her away from her entourage."

"Since when have you cared about the thoughts and opinions of humans?" Puck snarled at the thought of me becoming soft with these monsters.

"Since they started to matter to Titania," I confessed. The sound of the door opening caused both of us to quiet. We turned our attention to it, waiting for Titania. Around the corner came a string bean of a woman with thin blonde hair.

The unknown woman looked at Puck and me. Her eyebrows shot up, and she said, "Excuse me, this is the *women's* restroom."

I opened my mouth to speak, but Puck held faer finger to my lips to silence me. Fae looked at me and mouthed, "I got this."

"Ex-cuse me," Puck sassed before hopping off the sink. Fae walked up to the lady and held faer finger to her face. "Did you just *ass-ume* my gender? You know what they say about *ass-umming*, don't ya? It makes an ass out of you. So take your ass out of the restroom and enjoy the rest of your night before I make you squeal like the disgusting little piglet you are."

My jaw dropped damn near to the floor as Puck finished faer tirade. The woman's mouth mimicked mine, but she turned around and marched out of the bathroom. I looked over at Puck and raised my eyebrows.

"This is why I can't stand humans," Puck said before hopping back on the sink with me. "Their gender constructs are bullshit. They're so obsessed with the differences in genders and race, that they forget they are all human on the inside."

"Are you serious?" A familiar voice came from outside the bathroom door. Puck and I both turned our attention to the door, waiting for her to enter. I swung my legs, hanging off the sink in an anxious tick as I waited for Titania to come in.

The door flung open, and a click came from the door before she rounded the corner. Her glare, one I had been the victim of many times, drilled into my soul. I waved my hand at her and smiled.

"This," she huffed, "is CHANEL!" She punctuated her sentence by throwing her once white napkin in my face.

As the napkin fell to my lap, I picked it up and licked the wet ends. "Marroneto Brunello Madonna delle Grazie 2017?" I asked.

She snuffed a smile and looked away from me. "You owe me a blouse."

I waved my hand dismissively and scoffed. "I'll buy you another one." Taking a deep breath, I closed my eyes..

"Go ahead and say it."

"Let her reject you."

"Again."

I snarled and my eyes shot open. My breathing had intensified at the sound of the voices ringing in my head. "We need," I said between deep breaths, "to talk."

It was Titania's turn to snarl, as her bottom lip curled in anger. I knew that look all too well, and I also knew I was about to get the ass chewing of a lifetime. "Do you have *any* idea who is waiting for me at that table?" She demanded before approaching me and shoving a finger into my chest. "Do you have *any* idea what is at stake with this meeting?"

I rolled my eyes. "Some big wig director and your agent, I think." I snorted in pure frustration that she was so obsessed with her mortals. "They don't matter. We matter, Titania."

Titania sighed as she closed her eyes and lowered her head to face the bathroom floor. "There is no 'we' anymore, Oberon. We have been separated for centuries," she reminded me. She opened her eyes and snapped her attention towards me. "I have a family! And a career!"

"We told you she would reject you again."

"We know what is going to happen before you ever do."

"We know you're a failure, Oberon."

I slammed my hands on the counter I was sitting on, my strength causing it to crack. "But the world depends on us being one," I begged.

She rolled her eyes and scoffed, looking the other direction. "And people call me dramatic. The world seems to be doing just fine without us," she said as she turned her attention back to me. "Or as fine as could be expected, with mortals running the show."

I thumbed my nose at her. "You'd truly say the world is doing fine?" Titania looked down and away at my assertion. "That's why they need us. They can't do it themselves."

"They're doing fine enough for it to not be my problem anymore," she replied as she looked back at me with disdain written on her scowled face and narrowed eyes. "Besides, we did far more damage every time we fought."

"Our fights cleansed humanity!" I argued, sliding off the counter and moving towards Titania. "They needed it. Look at us, Tati. We've traded in the forest for concrete jungles, trees for skyscrapers, and nature for mortals."

She held a hand up to my chest to stop me from coming closer. She clenched her eyes and said, "Well, maybe *I* like it here! But what does my opinion matter to you, anyway?" I stumbled back in shock and rested one hand behind me on the counter as my back rested against the lip of the counter.

Titania stripped out of her blouse and carefully examined her camisole in the mirror to ensure there was no further damage caused by me. "You're very lucky that you only stained my blouse."

I sighed again, looking at the door as a woman entered the bathroom. She looked at me in disgust, so I did the natural thing and blew her a kiss as she walked by me. Something in the air caught my attention as my nose went up like a bloodhound's and I sniffed the air behind the mysterious woman. "Titania... do you smell that?"

"Ugh," Titania scoffed. "It's called potpourri," she sassed. "Now, would you get out before you bring any more attention to yourself?"

I rolled my eyes back in my head. "Not that," I said as my eyes came back to focus on Titania. I held a finger up along with my nose and took a deep breath. "*That.*"

Titania finally took a big sniff of the air, and her eyes went wide. "What is that?"

"You know what it smells like, don't you?" I asked her with a quirked eyebrow. Love-in-Idleness, the flower once used to hypnotize Titania into falling in love. That small white flower that the world thought Cupid had created. The very one Will wrote about in his play. The very flower that nearly caused me to lose her.

"And yet, you lost her anyway."

Titania cocked her head. ".... There's no way."

I moved from the counter and walked to the stall the woman went into. "Ma'am? Ma'am? What *are* you wearing?" I called as I banged on the stall door.

Titania's eyes widened, and she ran to my side. She grabbed my arm and tried to pull me away from the stall door I was banging on. "Can't you act normal? Just once?"

"That word isn't in my vocabulary."

The sound of the toilet flushing turned both of our heads toward the stall door. When it finally opened and the woman revealed herself again, she asked, "What the hell is going on here?"

"This... smell you're wearing. What is it called?" I asked her as I stepped forward to sniff the front of her shirt. I sniffed around her body to try to take in the scent. Once I was behind the woman, I looked at Titania and cocked my head to the side. I shook my head to confirm it was the smell we thought it was.

"Oh," the woman said with a disgusted face, looking at me as I sniffed the air around her. "It's from the debut collection of this new company, Apothefairy. It's called Love Sick. And I'm terribly flattered, sir, but I'm afraid I'm taken." The woman pulled a tabby cat out of her purse. "Yes, I am, aren't I, precious?"

Titania palmed her face. "Oh gods..."

"I'm taken as well." I smiled and looked over at Titania. "By this beautiful young goddess."

A scowl crossed Titania's face as she rolled her eyes. She pulled out a compact and blew dust into the woman's face. "Forget," she whispered. Titania turned her attention back to me. "Never do that again."

"Which part?"

"I am married," she stated with authority.

"Technically," I pointed out. "To me."

"No, not to you, Oberon."

"Pish posh," I replied with a wave of my hand. Titania stomped to the bathroom door, and I called out to her. "Wait, Titania." She stopped with her hand on the door, not turning to face me. "This doesn't concern you in the least?"

"Why would it?" She asked. "It has nothing to do with me," she shot back as she started to open the bathroom door.

"If that flower is being used to make perfume," I started. She paused and stepped back into the bathroom. "It certainly will be your problem when your mortal husband falls for the smell of another."

"You wouldn't dare," she challenged as she slowly turned around.

I gasped overly dramatically. "How awful would it be for him to fall in love with your ex-husband?"

Titania stormed over to me and grabbed me by my shirt. She shoved me against the counter, my back bent over it and my head planted against the bathroom mirror. "Do not fucking tempt me, Oberon."

I licked my lips as I looked down at her. "You're the one doing the tempting, dear."

"Stay away from me, my husband, and my family," she hissed as she let go of my shirt.

Defeated, I rolled my eyes. "Fine, I'll save the world by myself. Like always." I pushed past Titania and stormed out of the bathroom, stopping to lean against the wall just outside of the bathroom door.

"Told you."

"Failure."

"She hates you."

"She'll never love you."

"She never loved you to begin with."

"SHUT UP!" I shouted, causing the entire restaurant to go quiet as the patrons turned to look at me. I let my body drop to the floor as I pulled my knees to my chest and rested my head against the wall. I could hear a deep sigh come from the bathroom.

"You know he's a changed man, right, Your Majesty?" I heard Puck say as fae appeared in the bathroom. The crunch of an apple accompanied faer words.

"Not from where I'm standing, Puck," Titania answered. "He's still a hurricane that insists on uprooting everything I've worked hard for." I bit my lip as the words left her mouth. I shut my eyes and positioned myself to hear their conversation better.

"Or maybe," Puck started, taking another bite of faer apple. "He's working hard to re-root the very foundation he destroyed all those years ago. You know he hasn't been with a single man or woman since you re-married?"

It was true. After Titania's first marriage, I had been a hurricane and slept with every man and woman I came across. Once she divorced, I turned my focus to winning her back for a while, but I began sleeping with anything that moved and lost sight of her. Since she remarried the first time, I had been in a rut and wanted no one but her.

"He's poured his life into solving problem after problem," Puck continued. "Just so he doesn't have to think about all the ways he fucked up and lost you."
"Well," Titania said as she took in a deep breath. "Maybe he *needs* to think about how he fucked up and lost me. Cause he still hasn't learned how to show me any respect."

I spent the entire ride back home with the partition screen up. Bear knew better than to start a conversation with me when I asked him to pick me up in the alley behind the restaurant and had red wine stains all over my blouse. Of course, the freak thunderstorm that had kicked up during my reunion with Oberon was probably another good clue. *At least he didn't know about*

my separation or my new fiancé, I thought as I braved the weather. *I don't think California could survive the earthquake that would have caused.*

After a long drive of calming the weather back into reason, we were finally home. Bear helped me out and covered me with his umbrella as we approached the front door. Before we could open it, however, Sami had yanked it open. "Momma! Come quick!"

Oh, gods. What now? "What's wrong, my darling?"

"I think Malika's sick." That was all I needed to hear to leave Bear by the door to tend to the umbrella.

I followed Sami through the house into the kitchen. At first glance, nothing seemed particularly odd. Chad was cooking dinner, just as he said he would. Sami's math homework was scattered across the dining room table, which made sense since Chad promised to help her. Yet there was an awkward tension in the air. I could see Chad was stiff as he stood at the counter, chopping vegetables. There was also a pensive furrow to his brow.

The one thing out of place was Malika. I expected her to be filming her makeup reviews at least until dinnertime. And even if she got done early, I would have expected her to be editing the videos or managing her social medias or talking with her friends. The last thing I expected was for her to be sitting at the kitchen bar, watching Chad with such adoring fascination. With her chin resting in her hands, she was grinning from ear to ear as she watched him cook.

"She's been like this for hours," Sami grumbled up at me, clearly annoyed by whatever was happening.

Chad snapped his head over to me and Sami upon hearing my youngest child's complaint. He tried to suppress the sigh of relief upon seeing me and smiled. He had never abandoned any of his cooking projects before, but he left the knife and cutting board instantly to greet me. "Hi, honey!" The hug and kiss took me by surprise with their strength and enthusiasm. I mean, our relationship was wonderful, and the romance was definitely still alive, or else I wouldn't be engaged to the man. But it felt less like he was happy to see the love of his life and more like he'd just met a savior to rescue him from a terrible situation.

"Hello, darling. What's going on?" I asked.

"He's busy," Malika snapped from the kitchen bar. The aggressive tone called all of our attention towards her. Where the almost dreamy, big smile had been before, her face was now twisted in annoyance. If looks could kill, she would have given me the Julius Caesar treatment single-handedly.

"Excuse me?" A gentle rumble signaled the rain was about to get bad again. I could feel Sami hide behind Chad upon hearing my tone.

He put a protective arm around her, saying, "Hey, kiddo. Why don't you get your homework and we can work on it in your room?" Sami just nodded as she gathered her stuff.

"Oh, you don't have to leave, Chad," Malika cooed, her face and voice softening from aggression to flirtatious. "I'd hate for your delicious dinner to burn."

"Oh, it's fine," Chad answered with a forced smile. "I've got timers on everything, and all the prep work is pretty much done."

"Well, maybe I can come up and help too," Malika offered enthusiastically as she started to get up from the bar.

"Not one more step, young lady," I warned with a thunder clap echoing my command. Sami and Chad rushed upstairs and out of the kitchen.

Malika didn't move to follow, but she watched Chad go. Each step he took away from her looked like her heart was slowly being ripped out. And when he was finally out of sight, her eyes filled with rage again as she turned her attention back to me. "Nice job, mom."

"Would you like to adjust that tone of yours, young lady?"

"No! I wouldn't."

"Don't you raise your voice to me!"

"I'm an adult! I can do whatever I want!"

"Not for another three months, you're not. And if you keep yelling at me, you can forget about prom because you'll be grounded."

Malika crossed her arms. "Fine. I didn't want to go anyway."

Something was seriously wrong. "What has gotten into you?"

"What do you care? Since when do you care about any of us?" I was too stunned at the thinly veiled accusation to respond. "It's always about you and your career and your relationships and what you want. You couldn't give less of a shit about any of us. It's no wonder dad left you. And Chad deserves a nice, loving, devoted person like me who will actually take care of him. Not some bitch who will dump her children on him."

"That's it!" I yelled as a thunderclap shook the city of Los Angeles. "Go to your room and stay there until you can speak to me with respect!"

"Fine! At least the decent parent is up there!" And with that, my queen in the making stomped up the stairs, running to her room and slamming the door shut behind her.

With a heavy, tired sigh, I walked to the wet bar and pulled out the three bottles that were completely off-limits unless I was in a bad mood. Sparkling wine, passion fruit juice, and vanilla liqueur.

"Uh, oh." Chad's worried voice reached my ears. "Golden Glamour time."

"Unfortunately." I sighed, fixing the drink in a champagne flute. "I take it you heard everything?"

"We couldn't really make out the words, but we could definitely hear the yelling."

I sighed again. "Is Sami ok?"

"She's shaken up, but I had her put on her noise canceling headphones and take a break from homework."

"Where's Amira?"

"Still studying in her room." That was a relief. It meant that she was hyper-focused. Not even the long-overdue big earthquake could break her concentration. Much less a domestic between anyone in the house.

"I don't think either of them have ever seen or heard us fight," I said, shaking my head and taking a deep drink of my cocktail.

"Neither have I. I've never seen you fight with any of the girls."

"What has gotten into her?"

Chad shook his head as he wrapped his arms around me. "I don't know, babe."

"Did something happen while I was gone?"

"No. Everything was pretty normal until I brought her a snack. Then she started acting strange."

"What did you bring her to eat?"

"A parmesan chicken salad. Just the way she likes it."

"Could the chicken have gone bad?"

Chad shook his head. "I just bought it today, and it had a week left before it expires. And I would think there would be different symptoms other than just weird behavior. There should be vomiting or abdominal cramps."

"What else did she do while I was gone?"

"Pretty much what you saw. I brought up her salad, knocked when the 'recording' light turned off, and gave it to her. That's when she decided to follow me down here and watch me cook instead of finishing her make-up reviews. I was kinda happy at first, thinking she was warming up to me. But every time I looked at her, she had this... strange look in her eyes. And then she started making weird comments."

My brow furrowed deeper. "Weird how?"

"Let's just say that if the roles were reversed and I had made the comments to her, you probably would have called the police on me."

There were far too many strange things happening that day. It was all becoming too much. "Has this ever happened before?"

"Never. She usually avoids and ignores me when you're not around."

"Did Sami hear any of this?"

Chad shook his head again. "She thankfully missed the really inappropriate remarks. I think Malika adjusted and was a lot quieter after she came to work on her homework. But... well, you saw how she was behaving when you came in."

I finished my drink in one gulp. "I wonder if I should tell the girls' therapist about this."

"I think you should. They can probably figure out what's going on and how we can help her."

I nodded in agreement. "I'll call her tomorrow."

Chad gave me another squeeze and a kiss on my forehead. "Wait, what happened to your shirt?" He asked.

Oh, yes. The wine stain. "Ugh. Another stressful story. I need to get out of these clothes and take a long shower before I talk about it."

With another kiss to my forehead, Chad sent me off upstairs. "Go get comfortable. I'll finish dinner."

"Thank you, darling." How did I ever exist without such a kind-hearted gentleman like him?

I slowly climbed the stairs of our home. As I passed Malika's room, I slowed a bit. I couldn't hear anything, which briefly made me worry she had somehow snuck out, climbed down from her window, and ran away from home. But had that been the case, the security system would have gone off or Bear and his crew would have noticed her. Maybe I was just looking for an excuse to avoid another confrontation, but that was enough for me to move on and continue the trip to my room.

Before I could reach the master bedroom, however, a familiar fragrance stopped me in my tracks. I'd smelled the scent earlier in the day. At the restaurant. In the bathroom. When Oberon was... interrogating that woman.

I looked around to see that I was right outside Malika's film studio room. The door was wide open, and the film lights were still on. I stepped into the room, following my nose to the desk Malika sat in when she was filming her reviews. And there, sitting in a clump, were five bottles, all various shades of magenta. They all had a small logo—an 'AF' with decorative fairy wings on either side—and labels that read 'Love Sick'.

Oh. My. Gods.

5

Oberon

I sat swiping left and right, up and down on my table-top computer screen, trying to find connections to who-or what-may have been behind the creation of this new menace taking over society. Love-in-idleness was being used to trance mortals into falling in love. The problem? It wasn't just the single mortals falling in love; it was the mortals that were married or in relationships falling in love with people other than their partners. It would cause widespread issues across the globe if it continued. I had to find out who was behind the new 'Love Sick' perfume line.

The only connection I could find was that it was created by a company called Apothefairy out of Greece. With their headquarters being in Greece, I could only imagine that something supernatural was behind it. But who? Who would want to tear down the world I had worked so hard to create for the mortals? A world with less chaos and war than had been seen in times past, with science and technological advances out the wazoo. I guess when the king leaves his castle the peasants come out to hassle.

I turned on the television with the click of a button on my table. A newscaster and her co-host sat side by side as she talked about local politics. Her co-host, however, had his elbows on the table with his chin resting on his fists as he stared at the newscaster. I squinted at the screen through my glasses. I swear, it looked like his pupils had turned into hearts.

Pupils shaped like hearts? That was a surefire sign that Love Sick didn't just smell like Love-in-idleness, it used the essence of the flower in its formula. I looked down at my computer screen and swiped left to pull up the formula I had been working on to create a replica of the perfume. Going down the list of ingredients, I realized all I was doing was replicating the smell, not the essence of the flower.

"Wouldn't it be easier to just use the one flower we have left and create an antidote for that?" Puck asked as fae appeared out of nowhere. Fae sat on the couch with an apple in hand.

"Theoretically, yes," I agreed. "However, the ingredients in the perfume could nullify some of the antidote's ingredients, rendering that version useless. Then, we're out the only flower left in existence."

"That we know of," fae corrected me, lifting faer half-eaten apple towards me.

"That we know of."

But who could have gotten a hold of those flowers? Our kingdom was the only place they grew until we burned it all down a century ago. After Titania and mine's final argument, I had all the Love-in-idleness around the kingdom burned.

"I *can* use a petal from the flower and break it down to the molecular level and try to rebuild the essence," I suggested with my right pointer finger up in the air.

"Wait," Puck interjected. "If you can break it down to the molecular level, why can't you break down the perfume to the molecular level and duplicate it that way?"

"Good question, Puck." I glanced over at faer position on the couch. "And an answer I've pondered for the last fifteen hours. I *did* break it down to the molecular level and duplicated it that way already."

"So, then what is the problem? Why are you still working on the formula?" Fae asked.

"Because the scent was completely different," I answered as I pinched the bridge of my nose. "It almost smelled like a skunk."

"So, you screwed it up?"

"Ah, I thought that too. So I did it again. And again, and again. Until I couldn't take the smell any longer."

"I don't get it," Puck replied with a shake of faer head.

"I didn't either," I admitted to faer. "Not until I realized that Apothefairy was headquartered in Greece."

"Magic."

"Magic," I confirmed. "Whoever is behind this, has charmed the molecular structure to be different."

"So, science isn't so science-y?"

"Honestly, I have no idea what that means. But I'm going with yes and no. Science, at its core, is the root of all things. Science, or the theory of science, is what makes us, us. And humans, humans. Animals, animals. You get my point."

"So then, how is magic able to alter things at the molecular structure like that without changing what it actually is?"

"Magic doesn't *technically* change the molecular structure. It's more than likely an illusion charm that makes the molecules look different to a normal eye," I explained. "Illusion charms simply make things appear differently to the naked eye than they actually are. Of course, there are beings and gods who can see through the charms. Fae are not among those beings."

Puck chewed faer lip for a moment while fae contemplated what fae wanted to say next. "So science is above magic?"

"Science is simply a theory created by humans to explain things," I corrected. "However, humans don't believe in magic because they lack the ability to *see* it. It's the reason they believed the wind was caused by angry gods for so long."

"Ah," Puck said. "That makes more sense. Do you think humans will ever understand magic like we do?"

I clicked my tongue and stroked the black goatee on my chin in thought. "Maybe in another millennia or two. If they don't destroy the planet before then." I turned back around to the television as the phrase 'Love Sick' blared out of it.

"Love Sick," the television purred as the back of a petite woman with long, red hair cascading down to cover her bottom appeared on the screen. "Feel like you're the only person in the world," the voice finished, and the screen went black with a picture of the magenta Love Sick perfume bottle on the screen.

Something about that voice sounded familiar. I couldn't place why, but it made me scrunch up my nose when I heard it. The voice belonged to someone who made the hairs on my neck stand up. It had to be someone supernatural, but there were a ton of supernatural females who hated my guts. Whether because I broke their hearts or because I broke Titania's heart.

While the commercial didn't show any more than the back of the model on screen, she also looked familiar. Her hourglass frame was what any human woman would kill for nowadays. It was attractive, sure, but I preferred the thicker women with unshakeable confidence. It could have been the same woman as the voice, but I would hate for that voice to belong to a beautiful woman. Maybe the model was human and I had slept with her before? I didn't know.

A buzzing noise pulled me out of my trance. I turned down the television's volume and flipped over my buzzing phone. I almost wished I hadn't turned it over when I saw Titania's name and picture on the screen. *What could she possibly want?* We hadn't exactly left on good terms from the restaurant. Perhaps she was calling to follow up on my offer to buy her a new blouse.

"Hello, Titania," I greeted as I answered the phone. I took a deep breath and waited as the buzz of the phone line was the only sound emitting.

I could hear her breathing get heavy before she finally spoke. "I'll help you save the world." And the call ended.

# 6

Tati

I stood at the marble kitchen counter of the guest house across my backyard. The PR package from Apothefairy sat in front of me, taunting me with its logo. I put my phone down as quickly as I hung up and prayed against better judgment that Oberon would just accept my statement and not make this any more uncomfortable than it already was for me.

No such luck. My phone lit up and started scooting across the marble with every vibrating ring. "Jackass" flashed in big capital letters. An appropriate nickname meant to warn me to never pick up for him.

I sighed, picking up the phone and answering. I didn't say a word and thankfully I didn't have to. "What caused this sudden change of mind?" Oberon asked.

I hesitated, not wanting to give Oberon anymore insight into my personal life than what he already had. "Does it matter?"

"Everything about you matters." Damn that man. For all his chaos, all of his unhinged nature, all of his peculiarities, Oberon was a poet. He won me with words when we were courting. He won me back with them every time we fought until I was tired of pretty words that were never supported by actions and changes. Thank the gods I wised up, eventually. Otherwise, I would probably have fallen back into his arms and our turbulent marriage sometime over the last century.

I massaged my tense neck. "They got my daughter."

"Apotheshitty." The poet could also make light of serious situations without any warning.

"Yes."

"Then let's shut them the fuck down, Tati. We need to figure out the who and how behind all of this." Well, at least he was in a phase of doing as I asked without asking any questions. That would make this much easier.

"I have the PR package they sent her." I looked down at the only two words that acted as a return address. "Looks like they're based in Athens."

"That's what I was afraid you were going to say." So Oberon had been doing his own research since I left him at the restaurant. "This company likely has supernatural ties. They're not just run by some stupid mortal who lucked upon the flower."

"But who would do this on purpose? There's no way they don't know what the flower does." I put Oberon on speaker phone as I opened my smartphone's search engine and typed 'Apothefairy' into the search bar.

"Whoever it is has one of two things in mind: total chaos or a boatload of money."

I gave a mirthless laugh. "Why not both? They tend to go hand in hand."

Oberon gave a tired sigh on the other end of the phone. "You're probably right. And that doesn't narrow our list of possible suspects down."

My phone's search engine had come back with less than a page worth of results. Only one looked official and didn't seem to be teeming with computer viruses. It was the company's official website, and it was a single page ad for the Love Sick collection. No company information. No page about the CEO or the history of the company. Just a big button saying 'PRE-ORDER NOW'. "I'm not pulling anything up on Google. At least not about the CEO."

"I scrubbed the entire internet," Oberon replied. "They're clean as a whistle."

I looked down at the bottom of the webpage, finding the year of copyright and publication. "They haven't been in business for long. Looks like this was their debut product."

"An awfully good product at that."

I exited the search engine and went to YouTube, typing 'Love Sick Apothefairy' into that search bar. There were already half a dozen PR product review videos that had been posted. The oldest one was only a week old. And all the reviews were from some of the biggest beauty influencers on the platform. "They've sent it to every single high-profile influencer around the world. There are already product reviews up, and they're getting high view counts." Higher than what was typical, even for those influencers; a sure sign that the review videos featured some kind of strange behavior from the influencers after product application. "And they're getting higher views when they have weird behavior like stupidity brought on by artificial love."

"There have been more brawls amongst the high profile mortals over the last few weeks than we've ever seen. Just yesterday, I was at a party where Ben Affleck and Matt Damon got into a fight over Britney Spears. And she was wearing the scent."

I cringed a little, thankful that my family kept me away from a lot of those high profile parties. "Hell of a way to end her conservatorship. J.Lo must be livid."

Oberon chuckled. "Puck was there to console her."

"That doesn't make me feel better." Puck's version of 'consoling' left much to be desired and probably wasn't the thing that a woman caught in a love triangle needed after her fan-proclaimed soulmate got into a fistfight over another woman.

"So, how do we fix this?" I asked.

"I've been working on a replica using the last flower we harvested," Oberon explained. "That's another thing. We need to figure out how they got access to the flower. We kept them secret for thousands of years.."

"I'm sending my children away to their father's house for an indefinite vacation." That required more begging and congeniality than I was used to giving. But when I saw what needed to be done, I realized it was a blessing that Malika called her father to bad mouth and complain about me. It gave me the opportunity to keep my daughters safe and put some distance between Chad and Malika so that we could mitigate damage. Bradley having tabloid-level blackmail against me was a small price to pay if it meant we could save my daughter. "So we need to figure this out."

"Your husband's house?"

Oh, shit. "... Ex-husband, I suppose. Or he will be soon enough."

There was a long moment of silence before Oberon tried to console me "I'm sorry, Titania. Truly."

I genuinely couldn't tell if he actually meant it. Until moments ago, he thought I was still married and thoroughly unavailable. I expected him to be jumping for joy now that he knew my divorce made me available to be snapped up. At least he didn't know that Chad and I were already engaged. He didn't need to. We just needed to wait for the divorce to be finalized and then we could have the dream elopement on the beach the next day. If Oberon knew this plan was in the cards, I couldn't know how he would react. And as much as I hated it, I needed him level-headed and on my side.

"Just save my daughter," was all I could think to say.

"You have my word."

"What can I do to help?"

"Help me find a cure. Once we find that, we can sell it as a competing fragrance. Between your contacts and mine, we should be able to capture the same market as Love Sick with the cure. Then we find who's behind this and take them down."

"Okay. My family is leaving tomorrow. Where should I meet you?"

"I'll send a car for you. Just let me know when you're ready tomorrow."

"Okay." I was about to hang up when I remembered who I was talking to. "This is just business. I'm doing this for Malika. Not you." The king of the faeries was still a faerie himself. And all faeries were prone to mischief-making, and good at finding loopholes and lapses in people's boundaries and wards. So I needed to make myself clear from the jump.

"Whatever you tell yourself, Titania."

I sighed, too exhausted to take the bait and start that fight. "I'll see you tomorrow." Before Oberon could respond, I hung up. I took many long moments in the guest house to come to terms with the situation and figure out how to tell the girls about their impromptu trip.

"You're a failure, Oberon."

"*A complete and utter disappointment to your entire kingdom.*"

"*Such a weak, pathetic excuse of a king.*"

The voices kept coming as I walked down a dark corridor. Alone, the voices seemed to scream off the walls as they reverberated into my ears. I slammed my hands against my ears to block the sound, but the voices continued to beat away in my lost mind.

"She'll never love you again."

"She hates your guts."

"You're no good for her. You're like fire and gas."

"She's happier without you."

I fell to my knees and begged the gods to stop the voices. But nobody listened. In fact, I'm pretty sure I heard a cruel cackle coming from the darkness. I screamed into the empty halls, my voice bouncing off the walls and echoing eerily.

I collapsed, my face slamming into the dirt beneath me. My arms were spread out like a fallen angel crashing to earth. My back ached from the endless walking I had been doing, and my calves began burning and begging for a break.

"You're a murder."

"Murderer..." I whispered with a mouth full of gravel and dirt. "I *am* a murderer."

"You deserve to be hated."

*"You deserve to be **feared**."*

"Feared..." I breathed. "I should be feared."

"It's who you're meant to be."

I pushed myself up to my hands and knees. My head hung heavy as I heaved a ragged breath. Long strands of black hair fell across the side of my face. Slowly and silently, I lifted my head and looked ahead of me. In the far distance, I could see a tinge of light at the end of the corridor.

"The light at the end of the tunnel."

"You're too weak to reach it."

"Too much of a coward to fight us."

"A struggling child."

I put one hand against the brick wall lining the hallway and attempted to push myself up with my legs. With no luck standing, my body slid back down to my knees. I grabbed at the wall, hoping to find some kind of grip on the masonry.

As my nails scraped against the brick, scratching the tips of my fingers, I finally found a brick that was slightly ajar. I tugged on the edges of the brick to pull it out of place and slid my hand into the cavern where the brick once lay.

With all the strength in my body, I pulled up with my arm and pushed with my legs. My knees shook as my body slowly became erect. Once I was standing, I let go of the wall and began walking again.

My shoeless feet shuffled across the ground as I made my way to the light. I needed to escape the hallways of my mind. I was almost there. Once I was out, the voices would quiet down. I just had to make it to the light.

I stumbled and fell into the wall. Bracing myself with my hand against it, I took a deep breath. "You can do this, Oberon."

"No you can't."

"Yes," I corrected as I took another step forward, "I can."

I took one more deep breath and began sprinting down the hallway towards the light. My legs burned, but I didn't care. I had to get out and away from the voices. I couldn't stay there any longer. No matter how hard I tried to suppress them, they would just get louder.

I bolted up in my bed as I rolled around, twisted up in my own sheets. I kicked at them. It felt like the room was coming in on me. Heavy breaths escaped my lungs as I struggled and screamed.

Puck burst through the door of my room, looking around panicky. Once fae saw me, Puck ran to my side and shushed me as fae stroked my hair. "Relax, Oberon. It was but a dream."

With my eyes closed, I counted backwards from ten. *Ten. Nine. Eight.*

Puck's hand grasped mine and fae squeezed to let me know faer were there. Heavy breaths still made my chest heave as I tried to focus.

Seven. Six. Five. Four.

The breaths eased, however Puck's grip did not. A subtle reminder that faer would always be there for me, no matter what.

Three. Two. One.

I opened my eyes and blinked slowly, my breathing was back to normal. I looked into Puck's eyes and smiled at faer. "Thank you, Puck."

Fae nodded. "The voices?"

Always.

"Just a bad dream. I must have dozed off when I laid down to rest." I may not have been great at lying, but I was amazing at telling half-truths.

Puck nodded and let go of my hand. "I just want to make sure you're okay, Your Majesty."

I chewed on my top lip as I stared out the window. This city wasn't my home and I would be a fool to try to convince myself that it was. The thing was, though, the kingdom wasn't my home either. Titania was my home. She was the one I felt at peace with and I was never at war in my head when I was around her.

A tear slipped free and caressed down my cheek. Using the back of my hand, I wiped the tear away and looked back at my phone on the nightstand beside my bed.

I had a missed call from Titania and a new message from her. I swiped my finger across the screen and opened the message. '**They're gone. Send the limo when you're ready.**'

I looked over at Puck. "Send the limo," I instructed.

"She's actually coming?" Fae asked.

"She's actually coming." I grinned.

Puck took a deep breath. "Even though I know what your answer is going to be, I have to ask. Are you sure this is a good idea?"

"I need her help to do this," I responded. "I can't do this alone, Puck, you know that."

Puck nodded and left the room. I turned back to my phone and stared at Titania's message. I chewed on my bottom lip and took in a deep breath through my nose.

'The limo is otw,' I sent back.

That wasn't the first exchange that had taken place since Bradley and I had started the divorce proceedings. But it was the first time that I allowed him to come back to the house to do the exchange. To keep things civil, I promised to stay inside the house, away from him and his vehicle parked out in front. So long as he didn't enter the house, I would cause no trouble for him.

When the girls heard that they were going to visit their father the night before, their reactions were mixed. Sami was excited to see him again, and I couldn't begrudge her for that. The young one had so much love in her heart for everyone in her family, even if those family members were fighting. Amira was shocked in a neutral way, simply surprised that I'd allowed their impromptu vacation. She wasn't going to complain anytime soon, though. Where Sami's impartiality was from a place of love and care, Amira's was from the wisdom of knowing both her father and I were petty, imperfect creatures. And she knew that neither one of us were ever going to harm her in any way for maintaining a relationship with the other, despite our mutual loathing.

Malika was the most difficult to read in her mesmerized state. I could see the rage in her eyes when I had made the announcement at dinner the night before. She knew full well that the concession on my part was partially to separate her from Chad, the new item of her poisoned affection. And yet when Bradley arrived to pick the girls up, she was the first one out the door without so much as a 'goodbye' to me. She couldn't get away from me fast enough.

Malika's huffy departure left Sami and Amira confused and shocked. They both gave me goodbye hugs that were distinctly tighter and longer than was typical or even necessary for them to do at that moment. It was all I could do to keep my tears from falling. *I need to save my daughter. And fast.*

For the sake of my sanity and composure, I stayed far away from the windows until I got a call from the neighborhood gate attendant, assuring me that he had seen Bradley's car drive away with the girls. I removed my robe, revealing the unassuming outfit that I had hidden beneath it. I pulled my two large suitcases out from behind the lower row of clothes hanging in my walk-in-closet. The disguise was complete with a scarf wrapped around my head and tied under my chin, a denim bucket hat, and the cheapest pair of wide sunglasses I owned.

Puck's number was in my phone and at the ready. '**I'm ready**' was all I had to type. Within thirty minutes, Puck had made it through the neighborhood gate and was parked outside of my home. Of course, the limo that fae was driving completely undid all the discretion I was trying to employ with my ensemble. But at least the windows were tinted dark so no one could see inside. With the gate at the front of the neighborhood, no paparazzi would be able to sneak in and get pictures. So I would only have to worry about whether or not Oberon had that same type of security at his home. And knowing him as I did, he would.

Once I loaded my bags into the limo, I settled in the back and buckled myself in. The partition between myself and the driver was down, revealing Puck in a driver's uniform. "Hello, Your Majesty."

I rolled my eyes. "Hello, Puck." There was a long moment of silence and stillness before I ordered, "Well, get on with it!" Shifting into gear, Puck started driving us out of my neighborhood. "How is he?"

"Working non-stop. That's all he's done for the last seventy years. He works on this and that. He has no desires and rarely sleeps. It's one project after another."

"You will not guilt me into returning to him, Robin." Using Puck's 'government name', as the children called it, had always gotten faer to behave. At least when Oberon did it. Fae couldn't care less if I tried the same trick. But I still tried all the same.

"Not my intention. But you should be aware of what you're walking into, Your Majesty. Looking out for you, Catwoman." Oh, great. Fae must have been on another superhero kick. "You haven't spoken to or seen him in how long?"

"Not since Watergate, if I remember correctly." Gods, that mess.

"And was he at all his normal self then?"

Of course he wasn't. No one was. Not with what was going on in America at the time. "That's none of my concern." I wasn't his mother. I wasn't even his wife anymore. So I no longer had an obligation to worry about or tend to Oberon. He was a big boy. He could take care of himself.

"That was not my question." Always with the fucking semantics.

"He did seem thoroughly over the mortal mischief and bullshit." And he normally reveled in such chaos in the same way Americans reveled in the Super Bowl.

"That was before he revealed himself to the mortals and walked among them. Before he left the forest for good. Before he became the billionaire tech mogul, Obe. Now he's seen the corruption of humans. The fae has been working on ways to save humanity since the day after Watergate, for gods' sake. He's lost his mind. Prepare yourself, Your Majesty, for he is not the Oberon you remember. Neither the bad nor the good. He simply exists."

I didn't know what to say to that. What could I possibly say? Oberon's mental health had always been a little rocky, even when we were both in the fae world far away from the complicated and petty fights of the mortal world. Hell, my own mental health had declined since entering the mortal world, and I was, for all intents and purposes, the level-headed one in the relationship. I always wondered why he would leave the safety of the Faerie Kingdom for this world that was constantly being tossed about.

I pulled my phone out and began scrolling through social media. I needed something—anything—to keep my mind from wandering into destructive, hurtful directions.

"This isn't a trick, is it?" I asked Puck as the thought occurred to me. Manufacturing a love epidemic to get me in a position to reconsider our separation or guilt me into returning to my King was not completely outside of Oberon or Puck's realm of possibility. Nothing was outside of the realm of possibility with any fae really.

Puck adjusted their rearview mirror so I could see the frown fae gave me. "No."

"Don't look at me like you've never played a trick on me in your life."

"That is fair. But when it comes to Oberon, you know I don't joke. I can lie about many things, but to lie about Oberon is strictly forbidden by His Majesty." I could tell Robin was telling the truth. What I couldn't tell was if this 'strictly forbidden from lying about Oberon' rule was really set by Oberon himself or if that was just Puck's internal moral code. Oberon would forbid faer from lying *to* him. I can't see him making the rule of lying about him unless it was a lie that would make him look weak and fragile to his enemies. And any ruler or king would have such a rule. But creating a false catastrophe would hardly make Oberon look weak.

"What do you honestly think I can do?" I asked. "We were... we were terrible to each other. I believe the mortals call it 'toxic' these days."

"You most definitely were. And you both needed a break from one another. A break, Ross. Not a permanent new life."

"Ross? Oh, is this a reference to that stupid show?"

I could see Puck roll faer eyes in the rearview mirror. "It's one of the things the mortals got right, I'll have you know."

"And what about it did they get right?"

"It's comedy gold. A comfort show in dark times. A show that makes you smile."

I shrugged. "Whatever you say. I always preferred the messy sophistication of the Bachelorette."

It was Puck's turn to shrug. "The Bachelor was more my style." Of course it was. Watching a bunch of young pretty women tear each other apart over a mediocre man like a pack of alley cats fighting over a rat? That had Puck written all over it. I always preferred watching handsome men competing for the love and affection of a lucky young thing. I loved the idea of being adored by so many.

Before the conversation could continue, we pulled up to the gate of Oberon's home. Far sooner than I would have expected. He had been close by in his modern, art deco travesty for so long. And yet kept his distance. He had clearly gained some level of restraint and discipline since Watergate.

Puck punched in a code, opening the gates for us to drive through. "In all seriousness, Your Majesty." Fae looked at me through the reflection of the review mirror again. "Prepare yourself. Remember how odd Oberon was at the restaurant?" I nodded. "You're in his world now. This is his safe space, where he is himself. It's even worse. I thought about admitting him, but what would be the point? They'd either keep him forever or he would walk right out."

"It's not like you to be so sullen and dower." Or so hopeless. Puck could always find joy and laughter in the worst of times.

Fae sighed, pulling the limo up to the front door of the home. That serious look in the rearview mirror had turned to sorrowful pain. "Watergate was the last time you spoke to Oberon. When was the last time you spoke to me?" Korea or Vietnam. It was one of the two. But before I could say as much, fae got out of the limo, walked around, and opened my door for me. "He's waiting in the study. Follow the music."

I ran my hand through the ebony hair on the left side of my head and pushed it over to the shaven right side. Closing my eyes, I lost myself in the heavy techno music pulsing in my ears. I strummed my fingers along to the heavy bass beat as it thundered throughout the study. As I opened my eyes again, I glanced across the tabletop screen at the chemical formula I had created to replicate the essence of Love-in-idleness. The formula, for all intents and purposes, looked correct. I was just waiting on the machines to finish synthesizing it to create the essence so I could add a drop or two to the almost perfect perfume replica I had created.

A knock at the door broke my concentration. I yelled and pushed a thumb into my temple, "Just come in!" I heard the door creak open and the aura of the room instantly changed. My shoulders sagged as tension left my body and it went into euphoria. "Hello, Titania."

"What the *fuck* are you listening to?" She asked. She never was one for the pleasantries, always straight to the point.

"They call it electronic dance music," I explained to her. "This particular song is by Bassjackers." I closed my eyes and nodded my head to the thumping music as I turned around. Opening my eyes again, I saw Titania standing in front of me, looking mesmerized by the amount of pure stuff thrown around the study. Mounds of papers, several tabletop screens with drawings in dry-erase marker scribbled across them all, and the multitude of machines whirring along the walls creating new tests and hypothesizing new formulas.

She covered her ears in response and exclaimed, "Well, they're no Celine Dion!"

I scoffed. "Thank the gods, or I'd never get anything done."

"How can you even hear yourself think?" She asked as she shook her head in disgust at my musical tastes.

I sighed, half defeated and half not wanting to argue with her as soon as she arrived, and turned down the music. "It is all about moving the body to keep the mind working," I explained. I worked my body towards another table and started swiping on the new formula and moving molecules from one atom to the next.

"I'll take your word for it," she relented with slight hesitation as she made her way closer to the new table I was at.

Removing my tinted glasses, I wiped the lenses clean. Blinking a few times, I rubbed at my heavy, sunken eyes with the back of my pale clammy hand. Once my glasses were returned to my face, I stroked the five o'clock shadow that had begun to darken my jawline.

"Your room is to the left of this one," I informed her, turning back to look at the tabletop screen. "Puck should have your stuff up shortly."

She paused for a moment, and I could feel her hand lingering over my shoulder. The warmth of her hand disappeared before it ever made contact with me. "Thank you…"

I sensed her presence lingering behind me, and I turned my head to get a good look at her as I bit my lip. I couldn't help it. She was the one who made me feel at peace.

"But you don't make her feel at peace."

"You make her feel like shit."

"You look beautiful, Titania," I complimented her, closing my eyes to shut up the voices.

She raised an eyebrow and looked down at her gray Nike sweatsuit then back up at me. "I'm wearing a sweatsuit and baseball cap with no makeup on."

"Your natural beauty has always shone through more than the mortal standard of beauty you adhere to. To me," I confessed, letting out a deep breath as I opened my eyes once more to see her.

She pressed her hand to my forehead, assumingly to check my temperature at such a shocking statement. "When was the last time you slept?" She asked me.

"Last night." I smirked at her.

"For how long, Oberon?"

"A solid thirty minutes."

"When was the last time you slept for *more* than thirty minutes?" She sassed with an eye roll.

Without hesitation, I answered, "December 2017."

Titania sighed and turned around in an effort to leave the room. I could hear faint mumbles. "It's not my problem. It's not my problem. It's not my problem."

I spun back around in my chair and turned the music up, putting my head down like a scorned puppy. As I finished playing with the final formula I would need, I shouted over the music, "I'll spray you with the replica tomorrow and we'll see if it works! Get some rest tonight, Titania. We have an adventure ahead of us."

She stopped and slowly turned back around. "You already have it done?"

"The essence of Love-in-idleness is synthesizing now so I can add it to the formula I created to replicate the perfume. I just need to make sure it works," I explained without moving to face her. "The formula I made seemed to be right, but I didn't want to try it on random mortals."

After a long pause, she asked, "Then what are you working on?"

I turned around and smirked at her. "The cure."

Titania huffed. "Alright. That's enough," she grumbled as she came to the table and grabbed me by the ear. She began guiding me out of the room and down the corridors.

"Where are, ow, we, ow, going? Ow!" I managed to bite out between my declarations of pain from the pressure of Titania's grip on my ear.

"*You* are going to bed," she stated bluntly. She was acting like my mother, and I despised that woman. "Puck!"

Fae walked out of Titania's room and looked at her with a death stare. "I'm right here. No need to yell, Your Majesty."

I glanced up at Titania and saw her ignore Puck's sarcasm. "Could you prepare some organic chamomile tea with honey, please? And point me to the master bedroom," she requested.

Puck looked from me to Titania and replied, "I can do the first part. But, uh, you just dragged him out of the Master Bedroom." Fae nodded towards the door we had just exited. "He converted it into a studio years ago. There are only two bedrooms. A guest bedroom and mine."

I didn't need to see the glare Titania was giving me. I could always feel that glare Titania would give me without ever looking into the dark pits of her eyes. That glare would cause me to cower. "Are you fucking kidding me?"

I squinted at her. "If I ever needed to rest, I laid on the couch in the study."

Puck whispered, "Told you." Fae glanced around the room in a 'not my business' manner. I stuck my tongue out at Puck.

"Not going to cut it," she snapped. "Fine." She dragged me to the next room on the left and threw me inside the guest bedroom before slamming the door shut. Through the door, I could hear her ask Puck, "And I suppose he got rid of all of his pajamas as well?"

"My Queen, he sleeps nude," Puck laughed.

"Still?" She grumbled.

As I stood against the door, waiting for some semblance of a chance to make my escape, I snickered and asked, "Are you going to undress me too, Titania?"

"Not on your life!" She yelled back. "Now get in your birthday suit and get in the bed."

I hung my head and stripped down to nothing before sliding into the bed. I pulled the covers over my nude body and laid silently, listening to Titania and Puck's voices to help me fall asleep.

"Well damn. You did it," Puck said as they poofed back outside the door with the sweet smelling honey chamomile tea Titania had ordered for me. "This is the first time he has taken more than a power nap since Harry and Meghan's engagement party."

Titania let out a deep sigh.

"Believe me now?" Puck asked her.

"You'd think he would've learned how to take care of himself in the last century," she retorted.

Okay, that was kind of rude, Titania. I can take care of myself, thank you very much. I just choose not to.

"He cares more about taking care of the mortals than he does himself," Puck informed her. Fae were right. I truly wanted to help the mortals and fae alike create a more stable earth for all of us to live together in harmony. Would it ever happen? Probably not. But I'd be damned if I didn't try.

"How comfortable is the couch in the studio?" Titania asked. I wasn't going to have her, a Queen, sleeping on a couch. I started to get out of bed when I heard Puck clear faer throat.

"Take my room, Your Majesty. I'll sleep in the studio."

Titania replied, "Here is my credit card. Get yourself a hotel. You've earned a break."

I could hear Puck chuckle softly. "Thank you, my Queen."

"No room service. No hotel spa. And I swear to the gods if I find out you used the card to buy a sex worker, I'll hunt you down," she swore to faer.

"Scout's honor," Puck said before poofing off.

I heard Titania press her head against the door and whisper into the silence, "Why do you always have to do this to me, you old fool?" A tear slipped from my eye before I finally fell into a deep sleep for the first time in six years.

How I managed to get any sleep in Puck's room was a mystery; faer aesthetic was akin to that of a time traveler with ADHD or one who was slowly losing their mind. The water bed from the 70's was cold as fuck. The LED string lights from this century kept changing colors, and gothic decor cast unsettling silhouettes and shadows everywhere. And don't even get me started on the various paraphernalia that was scattered every-where.

I decided against sleeping in for the first time in a long time. I forced myself to do my regular morning shower routine, rushing through Puck's Versailles inspired wa-ter closest. At least the marble countertops and luxury bidet were more my style.

Once I was clean and presentable enough to allow Puck and Oberon to see me, I made my way downstairs to the kitchen. This was the one room in the house that was pristine due to lack of use. If Puck and Oberon ate at all, they either ordered out almost every night or had a diet made exclusively of the insane amount of junk food and snacks in one of the pantry closets. Oberon had always had a bit of a sweet tooth, but even for immortal beings like us, a diet of nothing but Ramune and chocolate caramel digestive biscuits wasn't healthy.

My guesses on Oberon's eating habits were further confirmed with a look at the contents of the refriger-ator. He lived like a stereotypical, blue-collar bachelor rather than a crypto mogul. It had been sometime since I had cooked for anyone outside of my daughters, and even then I had all the resources I could possibly want at my fingertips. With only half a carton of eggs and some cheese, my options were exceedingly limited.

Omelet it is. As I started gathering the ingredients and tools, I turned on the kitchen's plasma TV and flipped to the news station that was going to have the exclusive with Apothefairy's CEO. They hadn't had the interview yet, much to my relief. We needed some answers. And I needed to find some relief for the bad feeling that had been slowly growing in my stomach since I had realized they had gotten to Malika.

I took my time to make the omelet, not wanting to waste the ingredients that I couldn't afford to. If Oberon and I were going to eat this morning, I had to take my time and make it count. The news station was also taking its time. They knew that their exclusive interview held some interest to the public, and they kept teasing it before every commercial break to force viewers to stay glued to the TV. *Some people don't need to edge the audience to command attention.* Right before I finished the omelet, Oberon joined me in the kitchen, soaking wet, wrapped in a towel, and practically blind without his glasses. *What am I going to do with him?*

"Good morning," I greeted, flipping the omelet.

"What are you making over there?" He asked.

"Omelet. When was the last time you went grocery shopping?"

"A few days before I bumped into you. So, a few weeks?"

I furrowed my brow in both confusion and worry. "My, my. We have lost track of time, haven't we?" Whenever Oberon's sense of time was this off, it was never good. It meant that he was on the verge of a mental breakdown. And as destructive as mortal mental break-downs were, Oberon's could level a city. And it had.

I plated up the first omelet and slid it to one of the stool seats at the kitchen island. "No orange juice, sadly."

"I'm allergic, remember?" Oberon reminded me as he sat down, looking like a wet cat.

A rare streak of embarrassed guilt flashed through me. How could I forget? "Oh, yes. You're one for apple juice, aren't you?"

Oberon smiled. "I have a whole case in the base-ment?"

"Coming up next, the CEO of the startup company Apothefairy gives us an exclusive interview."

Finally, Oberon has good timing for once. "Puck?" I called out into the nothingness.

"Not so loud, Your Majesty." Oberon's assistant man-ifested behind me, holding faer head and looking like fae was going to be sick. *That hangover better not have been put on my credit card.*

"Could you fetch a new carton of apple juice from the basement?"

Puck groaned in exhausted pain. "But they're so heavy."

"You can get a Bloody Caesar on me if you do."

Puck squinted at me, indignant at my bribery at-tempt. "Et tu, Titania?"

I leaned over and whispered into faer ear. "Do it for him if you won't do it for me."

With another squint and groan, fae was gone. In a flash, fae returned with a gallon jug of apple juice. "You promised."

"I'm well aware. Just one, though." That was all the permission fae needed. Puck was gone back to whatever hotel room fae'd gotten for the night.

After pouring a tall glass of juice for Oberon, I settled onto the bar stool next to him, giving the plasma TV my undivided attention. "Who do you think it is?" I asked my former King. "It has to be someone we know."

Oberon peered at the TV, fighting his bad eyes as he munched on his omelet. "If it is, do you really think they'll just show themselves like this?"

I shrugged. "It depends on how badly they want to take credit for the chaos they cause."

Oberon shrugged back. "That's fair. I was thinking it's that Le Fay woman."

I shook my head. "Not her style. She hasn't been up to no good since she got married."

"Right. The bull-headed one. Such a shame."

"Why?"

"She's entirely too beautiful for him."

"Oh, but he's terribly sweet. And she needs a sweet man... bull. Whatever." If someone had told me Morgan Le Fay, famous witch and sister of King Arthur, would one day marry the minotaur from King Minos' Labyrinth, I never would have believed it. The faerie world was full of strange things no mortal could explain. That coupling was even beyond fae understanding. Still, she could do much worse. And I was happy for her.

Oberon chuckled at my diplomacy attempt. "So, who is your money on?"

I contemplated whether or not I should tell him the truth. But what would be the point? Either my suspicions were wrong and no harm would be done by the truth, or I was correct and he would find out anyway. "I have a pit in my stomach. I just really hope I'm wrong."

The music from the TV indicated we were finally back from commercials. That skinny bitch who was doing a story about me just 24 hours ago came on the screen. "Welcome back, America. She's a single mother, a scholar, and she's the CEO of the hottest new start up cosmetics company. Her first products, the Love Sick collection by Apothefairy, are already taking the world by storm, and they're not even out for general purchase. How does she do it all? Let's find out. Please welcome Mabel Carriage."

I knew what I was going to see the moment I heard the name before the camera turned its attention to Apothefairy's CEO. I frankly couldn't remember the last time I had seen her. She was clad in a white business suit, perfectly tailored to her thin figure. Her long, thick hair had been tied into a long fishtail braid that rested over her shoulder. And that makeup had to be her own work. She was always a perfectionist and would never allow anyone else to touch her face. She couldn't trust others to have her best interests at heart or the skills to meet her impossible standards.

The CEO of Apothefairy was Queen Mab. The midwife of the faerie realm. A faerie who particularly enjoyed causing mischief in the realm of mortal love and passions.

And my long-estranged sister.

I squinted at the television, trying to see better without my glasses on. Why did that name sound so familiar? Who was Mabel Carriage? I looked over at Titania, whose jaw was damn near on the floor. "Why does that name sound so familiar?" I asked before turning back to the television in time for the image of my archrival to appear on the screen. Shuddering, I thought back to the television ad that had all but turned me on. I dropped my fork on the plate.

"Well, shit," Titania said finally.

I sighed in frustration. Queen Mab was the last one I wanted to be going up against. I wasn't afraid of the tiny fairy physically, but she had a fucked up mind that would cause living chaos across the world. "She would be the one to be behind this," I grumbled as I shook my head. "She's so predictable with her antics."

"Fuck!" Titania screamed as she smashed her plate on the ground. She rubbed her forehead with a deep pressure that made me squirm uncomfortably.

I stood and made my way to Titania's side. I placed a well intentioned hand on her shoulder and felt the heat rising from her bare skin.

"Failure."

"She hates you, don't touch her!"

I took a deep, shuddering breath. "We'll stop her."

"Not with you involved."

"You'll fuck everything up."

Titania reached her hand across her body and placed it on my hand softly, careful not to give any wrong ideas to my already weakened mind. "How could she go this far?"

I scoffed at her question. Partly because I knew she wasn't going to like my answer, but also because she knew it was the right answer. "Because she's an evil bitch."

"She's still my sister," she replied, removing her hand from mine and turning to look up at me.

"I've never liked her, you know that," I reminded her. "Remember the first time we met?"

"Neither one of you made a terribly good impression that night," Titania shot back at me.

It was my turn to rub my temples with the pressure of a god. I grimaced as I recalled that fateful night. "I still feel like calling her a horse-headed, goat-titted heifer was appropriate."

Titania stifled a laugh. She knew I was right. I smiled at her and challenged her not to laugh. "Just as I'm sure she thought calling you a pig-headed, shameless, flirtatious madman was appropriate."

I nodded my head in concession. "As it probably was," I admitted to her. "I had no issue with that, but taking the last piece of bread was my breaking point." Titania could no longer hold it together and she let out a hearty laugh, shaking her head. "I don't understand how she got the flower, though, to create the perfume."

Titania paused as she turned her gaze away from me. "I might have told her what you did all those years ago."

"What do you mean, Titania?"

She sighed. "When you played that silly prank on me," she confessed. I gave her a confused look, mainly because I had played so many pranks on so many people in my past that I couldn't remember them all. "With

William." Ah. That one. "Turning him into a donkey and all that."

I bit my tongue and dramatically rolled my eyes. "Well, he was one." All I received in return was one of the most menacing glares I had ever been given. If I didn't know any better, I would have sworn she was staring at my very essence with those fiery eyes. But damn if she didn't look beautiful. I held my hands up and backed away. "Sorry."

She sighed again and turned back around, hanging her head low. "I needed to vent when I found out what you had done. My court wasn't cutting it. So I told her."

"So, she stole the flowers from me? It had to be before I burned them all." Whoops. Titania didn't know that.

"So it would seem," she sighed. When the realization set in, she perked her head up and turned back to look at me and quirked an eyebrow. "Excuse me? You did what now?"

I groaned. Cold, hard busted. "I burned the flowers after you left the kingdom. I decided if I couldn't have true love, nobody in the kingdom could have faux love."

"What a king you are."

"Hypothetically, we just need the flower that counters this one and then we can sell the cure," I offered. I wanted to quickly change the awkward subject we found ourselves on. "Between Tati Hastings' and Obe's backings, people will love our brand and counteract her shitty brand."

"Then let's get the flower to cure this stupid thing," she said with a sassy 'why-didn't-you-do-that-already' tone. Truth was, I had already sent Puck on the mission to find one of the flowers. I also wasn't confident that this would work. While in theory, the essence of one flower should counteract the essence of another, it doesn't always apply when there are other components and chemicals involved.

"Back to the forest then?" I winked at her.

Before Titania could speak, Puck appeared. "So you want the good news or the bad news first?" Fae asked us, looking at my half naked body and back at Titania, smiling.

"Get on with it, Puck," I demanded.

Puck rolled faer eyes as fae wanted us to play along with faer little charade. "Bad news: the flower that cures Love Sick is extinct."

Titania rubbed her head again, albeit this time in a much less gruesome manner. "And the good news?"

Knowing Puck, the good news wasn't related to our cause or really wasn't good news. "There better be good news, Puck," I said as I shot Puck with the same glare Titania had given me moments before.

"I found out who the CEO of Apothefairy is." Fae smiled and puffed up faer chest.

"It's my sister, we know."

I facepalmed as Puck's eyes dropped to the floor in shame. "Sorry, Your Majesties," Puck apologized before poofing an apple into faer hand and taking a mighty hunk out of it. I shook my head as the juice from the apple splattered my couch.

"Well, now what?" Titania asked, turning her attention back to me.

I shrugged my shoulders. There was only one thing left to do in my eyes besides finding the cure, which I was on the verge of. "We go find Mab."

Titania furrowed her eyebrows and wrinkled her nose. "What good will that do?"

"While we're there, we'll let Puck snoop around and see what fae can find for us. Maybe Mab has some cure flowers lying around. Like how Superman keeps Kryptonite." Her face never changed as she cocked her head to the side, staring intently and confusedly at me. I chuckled at her lack of comic book knowledge. "You keep the very thing that could destroy you. Keep your friends close and your enemies closer."

"I don't watch Marvel movies," she confessed. And what a confession it was.

I opened my mouth to talk. I closed my mouth without speaking as I thought better than to say the first thing to come to mind. "Ya know what, never mind," I mumbled.

"Let's see," Titania started, turning back to the television and rubbing her chin. "This is a live interview, which means she's in New York right now. Somewhere around Times Square."

I checked my watch and looked back at Titania. "We can be there in a few hours if we take the jet."

She shook her head and closed her eyes. "And she'll be on a plane back to Greece by the time we get there." *Check.*

"Then we just go to Greece," I offered. *Check mate.*

She let out an exaggerated sigh. Or was it a moan? "I didn't pack for Greece."

"Well then," I said as I smiled like the Grinch at her. "We can go shopping and then go to Greece."

She paused as she contemplated my offer. "I'll just go shopping in Greece," she countered. "It's better that we get a move on. How long until the jet is ready?"

"By the time we arrive at the airport," I told her as I walked towards the door. "Let's go."

"Oberon," Titania called out with a giggle. "Aren't you going to put on some clothes first?"

I turned beet red as I looked down at the towel covering my waist and my shirtless stomach still exposed for the world to see. "Right," I murmured. "Clothes first, then we go!"

I pulled out my phone and opened my active text thread with Amira. I typed out '**How is everything going?**'

A moment later, her response came in. '**Sami's having a great time, as usual. Malika is still acting weird, though. She keeps flipping between hermitting in her** room and moping around the house like the entire world hates her.'

'And your father?'

'It was nice to see him at first, but then he got called away for a job. His bodyguards are looking after us. Probably for the better. He was not handling Malika well. They fought a lot before he left.'

He spends months pestering me about getting to see his children, and then abandons them the day after he gets them? Some father he is.

I sighed, not knowing what to tell my daughter. What could I say that would make the situation better or even bearable? Nothing would get better until Oberon and I found the cure for the evil concoction. And even if we worked as hard as possible and used all of our other-worldly powers, finding the cure was going to take time.

'I'm sorry darling. I was hoping spending some time with your father would help.'

'Don't apologize, mom. Dad's always had his issues. I just can't figure out why Malika is freaking out so much.'

'I know. I hope we can figure out what's going on when I get back. Hopefully that will be soon. I love you.'

'Love you too, mom.'

"Careful with her stuff or I'll hang you by your sacks!"

Thank the gods I chose to text rather than call. The last thing Amira needs to hear is Oberon freaking out in the back. Or the jet.

As the airline employees finished loading our luggage, Oberon turned his attention away from them to me, his black hair whipping in the wind. "Shall we board?" He asked with the offer of his hand.

Switching my phone to airplane mode, I sighed and took Oberon's hand. "We should take off before my court gets here and tries to start a fight." There was no way they all hadn't sensed something was off with my children going to see Bradley out of nowhere and my recent radio silence.

"I think I'd like to see that fight." Oberon chuckled as he escorted me to the stairs of the jet.

"That's because you've not met Fern." I released Oberon's hand and held onto the stair railing. After only two steps, I stopped and turned back around to him. "I hope you brought something to help us pass the time." A fifteen hour flight with Oberon on a private jet with only the flight crew and Puck as company was a recipe for trouble if we didn't have things to distract us.

Oberon chuckled again. "I brought games." The question was, what games?

I continued my ascent into the private jet. The interior design of the jet certainly matched the crypto mogul persona Oberon had created for himself; black and grays with navy blues acting as the only pop of color in the whole jet. There were four seats facing each other that were pretty standard for business class. There was also a couch towards the back that I could easily see transforming into a bed with seatbelts. Mounted towards the front of the plane was a small flat-screen TV, and one was mounted at the back near the bathroom. And of course, the front of the plane housed a fully equipped wet bar.

I sat in the first seat I came to, facing my back towards the front of the plane. "Well, at least it's comfortable." One of the most comfortable airplane seats I'd ever sat in.

The plane door hatch slammed closed the moment Oberon stepped onto the aircraft. Rather than sitting down immediately, however, he stopped by the wet bar and pulled out two bottles of prosecco. He handed one to me before popping the other one. "To a new adventure." And like the spirit of chaos that he was, Oberon took a deep drink straight from the bottle.

I, on the other hand, fetched a champagne flute from the wet bar, pouring a bit of the champagne into the glass and placing the bottle in a spare bucket of ice. I took a sip and said, "Here we go, saving the world again."

"Just like we used to, only sexier."

"Well, we're the strangest members of the Avengers, that's for sure." At least I thought that's what that superhero group was called. "So, we go to Greece, and then what? How do we find Mab?"

Oberon paused his chugging to shrug. "I was going to ask you that. She's your sister after all."

"We haven't spoken in a century or so. That business with the royal family was a step too far for me." And based on recent events, I highly doubted my sister had stopped meddling with the Windsors after Edward VIII abdicated the throne.

"But you still have more knowledge of how she may react to seeing us."

"Oh, she'll get quite the giggle." I dug my manicured nails into the navy blue leather of my seat. "There's no way she didn't know Malika was my daughter. She sent it to her on purpose."

"No doubt. She wanted to poke the bear."

"Why? What did I ever do to her? Other than clean up her damn messes?"

"You did too much for someone who cared too little."

"That's why I put my foot down with Edward VIII." I was helping the rest of the royal family cope with her actions that led to King George VI ascending to the throne. And then of course, the Second World War hit and I had to spread myself thin for that too.

"But Mab is family, and I've rarely seen you stand up to family."

"Blood is thicker than water."

"And stickier. And you know full well the entire saying means the exact opposite of what you're trying to say."

I gave a heavy sigh and turned my tired gaze to Oberon. "What would you have had me do?"

"Stand up to the wretch like you always stood up to men. You were never afraid of men and what they thought about you, but you always cared about what the women in your family thought of you."

I looked down at my lap where I rested my glass of champagne. "It was just us for so long. I think that's why she gave you the third degree when you started courting me."

Oberon nodded. "That, and I've always had a reputation that followed me. Some fair, some not so fair. But they believed the worst of it. Only you saw the best of my reputation, Titania. Still to this day no one has understood me like you do."

I chuckled sardonically. "What can I say? I was going through my bad boy phase."

I wondered if Oberon would take the statement as a compliment or an insult when I said it. Fortunately, he laughed. "That explains Gancanagh I suppose."

That name made me cringe. "Oh, I forgot about him. How much of an idiot was I?" If Andrew Tate was of the faeries, he would definitely be like Gancanagh.

"Then I came along," Oberon boasted, puffing out his chest like a conquering hero. "Oberon, the true seducer."

"I certainly know how to pick them, don't I?"

"Up until me, you didn't," Oberon jested with a playful wink. "But aside from that ass, Will, you never went wrong after me."

I glared at him over the rim of my champagne flute. "What was wrong with Will?"

"Besides the fact that he tried to expose us to the world with that silly play, he didn't treat you like a queen."

"It was a beautiful play, and he was a sweet man," I argued back. "And he was funny. Very personable."

"Back to the matter at hand." Oberon's tone rarely ever got that stern.

I sighed. "Yes. Mab. She's never one to shy away from a confrontation, so I doubt she'll stop us from entering her office or building. She probably wouldn't even call the police if we started attacking her or her work. But you can guarantee that her workplace has so many security cameras and microphones that she could easily get blackmail material if we mistep."

"So we need a well-articulated plan."

"We're on her turf now. We need to get her into neutral territory."

Oberon smirked. "Luckily, we have Puck."

"You rang?" Came faer singsong tone from the couch bed at the back of the jet.

I leaned over the arm of my seat to get a better look at faer. "Does the fact that we're moving so fast make that at all difficult for you?" I hadn't used much of my teleportation magic since the automobile had been invented. So I'd never personally tried to do a disappearing and reappearing act in any form of transportation.

Fae shook their head. "It's like a roller coaster."

I shrugged, accepting the answer at face value. "I take it you're filled in on the circumstances?"

"I know all," fae replied with a shrug.

"Any ideas?" I asked faer.

"You go in to see your sister. Oberon will distract the guards. I'll get into the main server room and download the server onto a flash drive. Once we have that, we can get out and see what's on there. Surely there will be something we can use against her."

I shook my head. "Don't underestimate her. If there's one thing I know about Mab, she plans for all hiccups."

Oberon held up his finger, interrupting the conversation. "Which is why we're sending you in to see her. She intentionally didn't poke at me. I only found out about the shit by accident. Do you think she would ever in a million years plan on you teaming up with me again? After everything?"

I paused, trying to get into my sister's head to find the answer. "I would be surprised if she did expect it."

"Then we're already one step ahead of her. If we can find the formula on the servers, it will all be worth it."

"Do we have an escape plan?" I asked.

Puck pushed up from faer seat on the couch and conjured a roll of paper from thin air. Assembling the tray table between Oberon and myself, fae unrolled the paper, revealing building blueprints. "There's a helipad on the top floor with a perfectly functioning helicopter. I'm good friends with the pilot on duty today. I've offered him a job at twice his salary if he will fly us away in case of an emergency. Mab's office is directly below the helipad. The server room is four floors down from the helipad. No problem for me, I'll just phase. Oberon will have to take the steps."

Oberon groaned. "Isn't there an elevator?"

Puck rolled faer eyes. "Yes, but it'll take longer." Oberon pouted and looked away, mumbling something about working smarter, not harder.

"Well," I said, calling their attention back to the plan. "We can't fuck this up."

Oberon looked me in the eye, matching my energy. "We have one shot."

"Do we need a signal?" I queried.

Oberon looked up, contemplating, as he stroked his goatee. "What was that we used to say when we first got together?"

"'I hate you'? 'Fuck you'? 'Get lost'?" *Wow, we really were toxic.*

"Melinyet." The elvish word for "I love them."

"I suppose that will do," I conceded, trying to fight the heat in my cheeks. I did my best to hold my head high and hold Oberon's gaze. But when I caught Puck watching us with faer face cupped in faer hands, I had to look away in embarrassment as I sipped my prosecco.

Oberon cleared his throat. "Then it's settled. Once we land, you call your sister and set up a meeting time. Puck will disable the cameras and I'll distract the security while fae grab the server information."

I sighed. "This is a suicide mission."

"We have to stop her," Oberon insisted.

And he was right. "Yes, we do." Otherwise, Malika would be stuck in her lovesick delusion for Chad forever.

"We've got this, Tati. Together. Forever."

"It's been a while since we could say that."

"Even longer since we meant it."

This has to stop now before it goes too far. "I need to go to the bathroom." I stood up and made my way to the back of the plane, closing the door behind me before Puck or Oberon could say anything.

You're doing this for Malika. You're doing this for Malika. You're doing this for Malika.

13

Oberon

We made the rest of the plane ride in silence. I texted my connections in Greece, **'Be on the lookout for papz. Being followed.'** I laid my phone down and rested my head against the back of the seat. I couldn't figure out who, and had chalked it up as the paparazzi trying to find dirt on me. I didn't want to alarm Titania and chance her backing out, so I had kept this little secret between Puck and me for now.

My phone buzzed and I turned it over. Three text messages from different connections. Atropos was the first to text me back. '**10-4**'. Next was Clotho with a more inquisitive text that read, '**What kind of car? Looks? Anything? Come on Oberon.**' I rolled my eyes and moved my attention to the next text. Lachesis chimed in with, '**Will you come see me while you're in town?**'

I gagged slightly. I texted back to Clotho, intentionally ignoring the size queen, Lachesis. '**Black Honda, latest model CRV. Haven't got a good look at their face. Gender unknown.**'

Once we landed, Titania was the first one to cover her face with a beautiful white headscarf and shield her eyes with wide lens sunglasses. Once she stepped off the plane, Puck looked at me and clicked faer tongue.

"You're doing this to show her who you are now," Puck remarked.

I rolled my eyes and stood, gathering myself and stepping off the plane. The sun was bright, but I guess being so close to Mount Olympus and the God of the Sun, that was to be expected. I scanned the airstrip for any sign of the car I had ordered before we left. There wasn't a single car or another plane across the whole airstrip. It was eerily empty.

I pulled out my phone and dialed the driver's number. The phone rang until it got to a dead tone and hung up on me. Odd.

"Couldn't even do that right, could you?"

"Looks like we're going to have to order an Uber," I said as I walked down the steps. Continuing towards Titania, I finished, "My driver is nowhere to be found."

"Fuck." Titania spit as she pulled out a flap of the headscarf over her mouth.

I pulled out my phone and launched the Uber app, securing us a ride from the nearest driver. I chewed on my lip and flipped over to my recent call list. Pressing the call button on the driver's number again, I waited as the ringing sounded in my ear. Nothing. *Damn.*

"What's wrong?" Titania asked, turning her gaze to meet mine.

"Something is off, Titania." I looked out across the horizon. There was nobody around. It was like someone had closed down the airstrip and we didn't get the memo. I dropped my head after seeing nothing of note.

Titania paused. "Do you think she knows we're here?" She asked, a tinge of concern plaguing her voice.

"My driver *never* ignores my calls."

"Puck," Titania called out. "Any ideas?"

Fae appeared behind me and began, "I can't seem to track him down. I've checked all his normal hangouts." I rubbed my chin as I contemplated what Puck had just told me. "His home was ransacked."

My eyebrows furrowed deeply. "You couldn't have led with that?" Then, I heard a ringing coming from a phone near me. I turned to look at Titania whose eyes were filled with worry..

Puck turned to look at me as fae noticed Titania's concerned look. "It's her. Isn't it?" I already knew the answer.

Titania answered the phone, immediately switching it to speaker phone without saying a word.

"Tati, darling." There was the damned voice from the commercial. The one I had managed to avoid for a century. "Been too long, dear sister," Mab finished with a chuckle. "And hello to you, too, Obe. Congratulations on the crypto success! Oh, and don't worry about your driver. We just gave him a little spook."

I snarled at her voice and the cackling that preceded every sentence. "What did you do to him, you horse-fucking donkey faced hen?" I shouted as I took a step closer to Titania.

"Goodness." She scoffed. "You kiss my sister with that mouth? Like I said, we just gave him a little spook. Chloroform does wonders."

"Still all mightier than thou, I see." My nose crinkled as I glared at the phone.

"Stop me when I'm wrong, darling," she sassed.

"Oh, okay." I smiled. "Then stop. Is that all it took all these years?" As the words left my lips, a black limo pulled up in front of us.

"If I were you," Mab said, almost sounding offended. "I'd check that attitude. You want to have a chance at playing hardball? I don't negotiate with brutes." A man stepped out and opened the limo door to reveal Mab herself, clutching a champagne flute just like Titania did on the flight.

I caught Puck staring at Mab out of the corner of my eye. Fae winked at her.

"Mmmm," Mab hummed. "Hello, my little toadstool."

Puck blew her a kiss. I had had enough. I turned to glare at them and through gritted teeth growled, "Will you quit fraternizing with the enemy?"

"Oh, Oberon," Mab interrupted. "Fraternizing requires talking. Believe me, we can't get much of a word in when we meet up."

I saw Titania sheepishly walk towards the limo. Out the corner of my eye, I saw her slide into the farthest corner of the seat. I followed Titania, despite knowing full well this was a trick. Leaning forward, my finger trembled with barely controlled fury as I pointed it at her. "Listen to me, you bitch."

Mab lowered her glasses and raised her eyebrows. Her unwavering stare was almost intimidating. Almost. "Say it again." She smiled maliciously. "It sounded nice." As if off cue, the driver pulled us off the tarmac and onto the main roads.

Apparently, Titania was done with our confrontation. She screamed at the top of her lungs. "Enough! Both of you!"

I wanted to end Mab right then and there. I stared at her for a moment before turning to look at Titania. She was shaking with rage as she clutched the door of the limo. I looked back at Mab and ground my teeth. Clenching my fist, I closed my eyes and took a deep breath.

Mab took an obnoxiously loud sip from her champagne flute. "Mmm." She looked back at Titania. "Maybe there is hope for your husband, Tati."

"That's it," I started as I rolled up my sleeves. Before I could reach out and grab Mab by her long, fiery red hair, a bodyguard got in between us. He shoved a hand into my chest and forced me back into my seat. I struggled for a moment as I tried to escape his grip, but to no avail.

I sat back and dusted myself off and glanced at Titania. "How could you do this to me?" She asked, her gaze fixed on Mab.

"Oh, Tati." Mab waved dismissively. "Don't be so dramatic. Not everything I do is to spite you. You're not the center of the universe."

"Then why?" I questioned Mab.

"You knew Malika was my daughter!" Titania shouted across the limo, her body trembling as the rage pulsed through her limbs. "You absolutely did this to hurt me!"

Mab shrugged in reply. "I thought it would make for a good laugh."

"You're sick, Mab." I clenched my fist as I glared daggers at her relaxed expression.

Mab rolled her eyes and looked away from me. "Says the man who was so threatened by a mortal he turned him into a donkey."

Titania ran her hands through her short hair, clearly frustrated that we were getting nowhere besides further spun into Mab's web. "And once again, I have to clean up the mess from you having a good laugh, Mab."

"No one's asking you to clean up anything, Tati," Mab remarked. "Why not just sit back and enjoy the show?"

"Because my child is in love with my fiancé!" Titania screeched with tears streaming down her face. I sucked my teeth as I took in the new information. I knew something had impacted Titania, but I thought it was just the divorce. This, though, was totally too far. Even for Mab.

"Goodness," Mab replied as she placed one hand on her chest and widened her eyes. "Have you always been threatened by your own children?"

"He's a grown man!" Titania screamed, covering her ears. "She's still a child! And it's not real! It's all a hallucination created by your poison."

"Well," Mab laughed. "I needed to make sure he wasn't a creep. If he's going to be the new father of my nieces. No offense, Tati, but you don't make good choices when it comes to your partners." Mab glanced in my direction and rolled her eyes at me before turning back to Titania.

"Oh, that's it." I had had enough. I pushed past the bodyguard sitting beside Mab and grabbed her by the shirt. With one hand pushing the bodyguard into the door, I pulled Mab nose to nose with me. "Stop."

"Excuse me," Mab huffed, clearly offended that I had even touched her. "This is Chanel."

"*Excuse me, this is Chanel,*" I mocked her pretentious attitude. The same bodyguard that had manhandled me back at the airstrip reached his large hand across my shoulder and slammed me back against the seat. The movement forced my hands to release Mab's blouse and rip the material in trying to take her with me.

"Tell us how to counter your stupid little trick," I demanded as I brushed off my shoulders.

"Why would I tell you how to undo my master plan?" Mab snarled.

"Worth a shot," I shot back with a shrug. "What do you want from us?"

"Oberon, darling," Mab cooed as she waved her hand at me. "All due respect. You have nothing I want. Tati knows what I want."

I turned and arched an eyebrow at Titania. She let out a heavy sigh and looked away from us both. "We both know no one is ever going to be good enough for you," Titania said wearily. "So why bother trying anymore? Besides, your approval of my relationships are unnecessary."

Mab smirked. "You forget who I am."

"You may be a queen, my dear sister," Titania said, shifting her gaze back to Mab with the fire of a thousand hell storms. "But I am *the* Queen. And I am *your* Queen." My eyes went wide as she spoke with authority for the first time in years. "You will either put this right, or you will be added to our list of traitors and war criminals."

"Being a member of the royal family allows me diplomatic immunity, Tati." Mab let out a maniacal laugh. "You know that."

"And if I disown you," Titania pointed out, "you won't be a member of the royal family anymore and your diplomatic immunity will be revoked." I held my balled up fist straight out and opened it, mimicking the dropping of the mic.

"Then do it." Mab smirked and rolled her eyes at Titania's challenge. "Disown me. Right here. Right now. Go on, I'm waiting." Titania fell silent as she stared at her sister with hurt in her eyes.

"Okay, look," I interjected. "This is getting out of hand. Mab, you need to quit. This is going to hurt innocent people."

"Mortals." She shrugged. "Hardly innocent. Don't tell me that all those years in L.A. have made you both blind to the crimes of humanity."

"It's our responsibility to guide them," I ground out through gritted teeth and punched the door. My fist collided with the metal that buckled underneath my force and pain jetted up my arm to down my spine.. "The crimes of humanity are on our hands!"

"Your hands," she reminded me. "Not mine. I didn't take part in this weird adoption agency you two have had going for centuries. Me, I do my thing. Pull a couple of heart strings, stiffen a few cocks, facilitate a few misunderstandings."

"Be a massive bitch," I added.

"Mmmm," Mab purred. "Now you're just *trying* to turn me on, Oberon. It's a very good thing that Tati's engaged. I would hate for a man to come between us."

"Oh fuck off," I muttered, rolling my eyes and looking away from Mab. "I'm far from interested in you."

Titania let out a defeated sigh and commanded, "Pull over."

"We're not at your hotel yet," Mab said with a quirked eyebrow.

"Pull. Over," Titania grit out as she balled up her fists and her body began shaking.

I slid my knife from my waist and lunged forward. The bodyguard's hands swiped at me, but I was too quick. Leaning over the open partition to the driver, I placed the blade of the knife to his throat and brought my lips to his ear. "Third time's a charm."

The driver pulled over without an order from Mab, at the threat of death. Titania got out of the limo in such a hurry that she sacrificed her disguise from the paparazzi. Aimlessly, she took off down the road.

I jumped out of the car and gathered our stuff from the trunk. Poking my head back in the car, I said, "I hope you're happy, you pig-faced whore."

"Why don't you ask yourself how you could have stopped this, donkey boy?"

"By killing you years ago." I spat in the limo and ran off, calling Titania's name.

I t wasn't Oberon's voice calling to me as he pursued me that stopped me in my tracks. It was sheer exhaustion. Even by the standards of my daily norm, the last few days had been far too stressful. I worried about Malika. I worried about Chad. I worried about what poison my ex-husband had been pouring into my children's ears before he left. I was worried about all of my children only having some body guards to keep them safe. I worried about the tabloids catching me anywhere in the presence of Oberon. And now, I had to contend with the fact that the culprit for almost all of these terrible situations was my own sister. It was all becoming too much. My heart rate had been elevated since I woke up, and my body was crumbling under the stress.

I sighed, leaning against the nearest wall to catch my breath and try to calm myself. A migraine had started to form, and I wanted to keep the throbbing pain from growing any worse.

Oberon dropped our luggage unceremoniously and came over to me with outstretched arms. I didn't return the embrace. The move was punctuated with a tender kiss to my forehead. The forehead kiss lasted a little too long to be appropriate for long-estranged, divorced spouses. But I didn't care at the moment. I was exhausted from pretending that I was keeping it all together.

"Why can't I ever do it?" I asked, partially rhetorically and partially looking for an answer.

And classic Oberon instantly had an answer. "Because despite everything, she's your sister. She wasn't too wretched growing up." I was too tired to be surprised that Oberon had actually paid Mab his version of a small compliment. "It wasn't until she lost the title to you."

15

Oberon

I leaned against the beige wall and rolled my eyes. We had *finally* made it to the hotel by foot and Puck just couldn't wait to take a piss, so we came back to the room. A quick chat with the Fates alerted me that I was still being followed. It was almost like whoever was tailing me was one step ahead of me at all times. I had to find out who was tailing me, without Titania noticing first. There was no need to freak her out even more. "Come on, Puck," I hissed as I beat on the bathroom door fae were in. "We don't have all day. Who knows when Titania will be back."

The toilet flushed, and Puck opened the door. Fae rolled faer eyes and pushed past me. "What do you care if she knows you're gone, anyway?"

"Yeah, Oberon, what do you care?"

"Not like she cares about you."

"Failure."

I squeezed my eyes shut and turned around to face Puck. "Because I don't want to freak her out."

"Yeah, because you don't do that already."

"She's going to find out eventually. She isn't an idiot," fae reminded me. "She may have gotten soft in her time around the mortals, but she hasn't gotten stupid."

"Stupid, no," I stated, opening my eyes. "But she hasn't always been the most aware." Puck raised an eyebrow at me. "Think about how many times we snuck around and followed her and she never noticed."

"That we know of," fae said as fae held up faer finger. "Plus, we're magical beings. Of course, it would be hard for her to track us."

"And if this being following us is also magical?" I questioned as I pointed my finger in faer face.

"Then you never would have seen them. You're a failure."

"Failure."

"Failure!"

Fae brushed my hand away and rolled faer eyes. "Chances of that are slim to none. If that was the case, don't you think you wouldn't have seen them?"

"Unless they're reckless. Which would fit Mab's crew's M.O." I reminded faer.

"Then we're right back to where we began." Fae threw up faer hands. "Why are we sneaking around if this being is careless and will probably get caught by Titania, anyway?"

I pressed my pointer fingers into each of my temples and huffed. "Will you, for one minute, stop being sassy with your hands? With Titania being so stressed, she's even less aware of her surroundings than usual."

Fae waved faer hand at me and grabbed a brown coat off the chair. Puck threw it around faer slim body and ruffled faer hair with a huff. "Are we going or what?"

"Sass," I pointed out and opened the door. When I motioned my arm towards the door, Puck nodded at me and walked out.

When we got to the elevator, fae turned to me after pressing the down button and asked, "So, when was the last time you saw this mysterious person? Have you even seen them in Greece?"

As the elevator dinged and the door opened, we stepped inside. "They were in a bodega across from where we stopped in the limo."

Puck raised an eyebrow while the door of the elevator closed, and we began our descent. "And they've been following us since L.A?"

"Since the first night that I 'bumped' into Titania at that restaurant," I confirmed. "They were in an alleyway when I came into the restaurant and across the street when I left."

"How can you be sure it was the same person?" Puck asked. That was a fair question.

"Because I'm sure. That's how."

"You've always been paranoid."

"That's what made you a failure as a king."

"You couldn't even keep her thanks to all your paranoia."

"Failure!"

The ding of the elevator canceled out the voices as I took a deep breath and stepped out of the elevator. Puck followed closely behind. I made my way out of the hotel, scanning every alleyway and opening within sight to catch my predator. I made it my mission to find that mysterious figure.

Puck sighed and said, "Your Majesty, with all due respect, you have been known to be paranoid when it comes to Her Majesty. If I may remind you, you started an entire war with another kingdom because you thought a member of their court was courting Titania."

"We still don't know if that punk was or wasn't," I reminded fae as I pointed a finger in the air to stop Puck in faer tracks. Lowering my voice, I whispered, "Don't look now, but we're being followed."

Puck stopped and turned around. "Fucking Puck," I mumbled as I turned around as well. A shadowy figure behind us ducked into an alleyway. I could hear heavy footsteps running. "See what you did? You've spooked them off. They know we're onto them now."

"Run, idiot."

I took off running, leaving Puck behind. I turned the corner and ran into the alleyway. That was when I realized it was a human man climbing the fence. How do I know he was human? Because no magical being his height would have to climb a fence. They'd either be able to jump, float, or walk right through it.

I took off into a full sprint after the man. I heard Puck calling from behind me, begging me to wait up. But I didn't care. I had one goal in mind; it was to find out who was following me.

The man turned to look at me from atop the fence. His hazel eyes widened with fear. Whoever he was, he knew who and what I was.

Falling once he got over it to the other side, A black strap hanging around his neck was hung on the fence. I took that as my opportunity to catch up to him and took off into a full-blown sprint. His eyes widened again and he yanked on the strap. I watched as it ripped and the strap around his neck fell to the ground with a cracking sound. He took off running and rounded another corner onto the street.

I leapt over the fence like an Olympic hurdler. I hit the ground with a thud, cracking the concrete underneath my feet with my hand flattened on the ground to catch my fall. Pushing forward, I rounded the corner onto the street. Either way I looked, trying to find him, it was nothing but a crowd of people.. "Fuck," I spat. I would never be able to find him.

I turned and kicked the wall of the building beside me. The building shook and a few loose pieces of brick fell from the wall and smacked me in the head.

A hand touched my shoulder, and I spun around, grabbing the person's wrist and twisting it in the most painful way possible. Once I got a look at the person who invaded my space, I realized it was Puck. In faer hands was a black camera.

"Where did you get a camera from?" I asked, snatching it from faer hands and turning it on.

"Whoever you were tailing dropped it." Fae showed me the black ripped strap that had been holding the camera around the human's neck.

I tried to scroll through the pictures on the camera but was greeted by a message of 'No Memory Card'. I threw the camera down on the ground and it shattered into pieces.

Puck looked at me wide eyed and asked, "Now, just why did you do that? That was our only clue."

"Because, Puck," I growled, looking up at fae. "He took the memory card out before he dropped it. Nothing's on it."

"Well, at least we know you're not just being paranoid," Puck muttered, leaning down to pick up the shattered camera.

I scrunched my nose and faked a laugh. "We can't tell Titania," I said. "Not yet, anyway."

"Why?" Puck questioned me, returning to faer erect position.

"She'll freak out if she knows someone with a camera is following us."

"Did you at least get a good look at the guy?" Puck asked hopefully.

I shook my head and looked down at my feet. I was blinded with rage while I was on the chase. "Brown hair and hazel eyes are all I know. He looked familiar, but I couldn't place him."

"Paparazzi?"

"That's what I'm thinking," I admitted. "But who would be interested in me?"

"A failed king."

"A failed husband."

"A failure."

"You're a billionaire tech mogul with an air of mystery. Half the world is interested in you," Puck reminded me. I shook my head to clear the thoughts and looked back up at fae. "And if someone saw Titania leave and stalked her to your place, well…"

"We need to find him before he reports to whoever he's working for. It'll freak Titania out too badly and she'll leave." I sighed.

"Again."

"Again," I added.

"Oberon, look," Puck said as fae pointed at something on the camera with a raised eyebrow. "There are initials on the bottom of the camera in silver marker."

"What are they, Puck?" I asked, rather impatiently.

"BF."

"Bradley Fletcher." My jaw dropped at the realization.

"Who?" Fae asked with a scrunched up nose and furrowed brows.

"Titania's ex-husband."

Fuck. Me.

16

Tati

I finally composed myself enough to put my disguise back on. It either worked, or everyone in Athens was far more polite than they were in America. No one approached me with phones and cameras demanding pictures and autographs. I was left alone to do my shopping and dwell on my thoughts.

I took my time as I walked through the streets, taking in the sights of my old home. So much had changed in the last several centuries. Those simple neighborhoods and craftsmen and families had expanded into tourist attractions, eradicating the nature Oberon and I once sought to protect. The good feeling that I thought I would get from shopping was severely overwhelmed by the sadness I felt at my own nostalgia. The Athens of my youth and childhood was gone forever. It would never come back.

Could I have stopped this? Could we have stopped this if we both had just stayed? I didn't know. I couldn't know. Immortality gave me many perks and senses mortals couldn't comprehend, but only a chosen few could see the future and see every possible timeline and outcome of every single choice. I had lost track of those few. Even if I could find them, there was no guarantee they would talk to me. And even if they did, their conversation would primarily be made up of riddles, as was typical of their archetype.

It truly was a mental prison that I'd gotten myself into. I wanted to know if things would be better if I had made different choices. But what good would it do to know? I couldn't go back and change the past. I would just have to live with the guilt of my choices and behavior and commit to doing better in the future.

The only thing that pulled my mind from the dark, depressing thoughts that were creeping up was the familiar, warm smells filling my nose. Where American mortals were comforted by the scent of their mothers' secret chocolate chip cookie recipes, the smells of warm falafels, gyros, Greek pies, and koulouria were what took me back to simpler, happier times.

I followed my nose to a bakery with their door wide open to welcome tourists, manage the heat, and tempt hungry stomachs. Even though it was the middle of the afternoon, the pastries and baked goods still smelled fresh out of the oven. I moved slower than I had in a very long time, taking in all the sights and smells of the perfect food before me.

"Good evening, sweetheart." I looked up to see an older Greek woman. She was the exact type of person Lainie Kazan would have modeled her character after in those movies. The one all about the adult daughter finally getting married to a non-Greek boy. "Can I help you?" The woman asked, still speaking Greek.

"Yes," I responded, also in Greek. "Can I get three trigona panoramatos, two spinach kalitsounias, a diple, a severing of loukoumades, and three tiropitas?"

The woman's eyebrows had shot up over the lengthy order, but she began collecting the pastries, assembling them into a box as I called them out. "Would you like a bag?"

"Yes, please."

With a flick of the wrist, I turned all the American dollars in my purse into euros and handed them to her, paying for the food. Yes, it was expensive, but handmade Greek pastries made from scratch were well worth the price. "Come again, sweetheart."

"I will," I called with a smile, walking out of the store. It was going to take all of my discipline to get back to the hotel without sneaking a bite, but I would do my best. Besides, both Oberon and Puck would kill me if they saw that I started without them.

With my feet more firmly planted on the earth and head back on straight, I started the walk back towards the hotel. I didn't even need my phone's GPS to get on the right track. Even with all the changes that had taken place over the years, I knew exactly where I was trying to go. Maybe not by logical geography, like street names and kilometers, but I knew by visual and memorized geography. Sights and feelings.

On my way back to the hotel, I couldn't help but turn my attention to what seemed to be a luxury shop. It didn't bear the name of any commonly known luxury brand like Gucci or Louis Vuitton, but had similar vibes just from the look of the outside. It was simply called '□□□□□□□' or 'Sirens'. A tempting name for a tempting store.

Before I could even stop myself, I was stepping out of Athens' heat and into the air-conditioned space of 'Sirens'. The rustic style of Greece was forced to give way to sleek, clean, modern shapes and lines in monochromatic black and white color schemes. The store looked like someone had taken every American mall's multi-level department stores and condensed them into a single store. One side was dedicated to feminine luxury clothing. The other side was masculine luxury clothing. And the middle of the center aisles of the store was dedicated to makeup, perfume, and cologne.

A glimpse around the store showed that all the clothing items carried the same monochromatic look as the store's interior design. It was all white, black, brown, and beige in blouses, dress pants, dresses, boots, and heels. It was the same in the masculine luxury clothing section, just in suits, dress shirts, sports jackets, dress pants, loafers, and socks. As a woman who preferred to don herself in as many colors as possible, nothing particularly appealed to me.

About the only section in the store that I found appealing was the makeup and perfume section. Surely I could spare some money to get myself a small present for all the trouble I was going through with this whole ordeal? The question was, what should I choose?

I decided to start with the perfume. I picked up every sample of feminine perfume, spraying them on the sample cards provided to test them out. The smell of flowers and artificial fruit flavors assaulted my nose, nearly making my eyes water. There was no gentle finesse to them. *Do the manufacturers believe that the most obnoxious scents are the way to attract buyers and their lovers?*

I was so deep in my critical thoughts that I didn't realize I had picked up a familiar magenta bottle until I sprayed the liquid and inhaled the scent. I immediately froze as the perfume struck a familiar nerve in my mind and memory. A slow look at the bottle revealed my worst fear. I had just inhaled the smell of Love Sick. The wretched creation of my sister.

"Fuck," I hissed under my breath. *What should I do? I couldn't risk looking at anyone lest I fall under my sister's spell.* But how was I supposed to avoid looking at people? The streets of Athens were teeming with people, and they would stay that way until late into the night. I could try to navigate the city with my eyes fixed on the GPS. But that could get me run over if I had to cross a busy street *I need to call Oberon. He'll find a way. Maybe he can come pick me up. I just have to not look at anyone—*

A young voice called out in greek, "Good evening, Madame. Can I help you find something?"

Before I could stop myself, my reflexes pulled my head up to look at the speaker. A young woman, probably in her late twenties at the oldest, wearing items from the store's very racks. She was a classic Greek beauty with long, dark hair styled into gentle, beach wave curls. She wore just enough makeup to accentuate her pleasant features and hide any possible blemishes. It wouldn't surprise me if she didn't have any. She had over half a foot on me in height, and her petite, lithe body suggested a background in dance. Her brown eyes were warm with golden undertones, almost cat-like in their focus.

She was absolutely gorgeous.

And I felt absolutely nothing for the woman at that moment. Not a single butterfly flew through my stomach. My heart didn't skip a beat, and I didn't feel any heat rising to my cheeks.

I felt none of the things I felt when I fell in love with the donkey form of William Shakespeare under the effect of the flowers all those centuries ago. I felt normal.

"Ma'am?" The girl asked in concern at my staring silence. "Are you alright?" I pulled my gaze away from her down to the sample bottle of Love Sick that was still in my hand.

I was immune to my sister's diabolical creation.

The door to the hotel room crashed open. "Oberon!" I heard a voice call from deep within my sleep. My eyes fluttered open as I tried to clear the sleep from them and see who was calling my name. "Oberon!" Titania called again.

I jumped from the couch and ran to her. "What?" I asked, taking her in my hands and examining her at arm's length to ensure she wasn't hurt. "What's wrong, Titania?"

Out of breath, like she had just run a marathon, Titania huffed and puffed, trying to catch her breath in between words. "It... doesn't... work... on me."

I arched an eyebrow and searched her face. I knew she could see the confusion on my face clear as day as she shut her eyes and shook her head. "What are you talking about?"

"Love Sick..." she finally got out. "It doesn't work on me."

"What?" I asked, my jaw dropping.

"I don't fall in love when I use it." She confirmed.

Suddenly, a heat flushed and reddened my cheeks. A pit formed in my stomach as I straightened my back. I let go of her arms and brushed off the front of my shirt.

"Awww, is someone jealous?"

"And just how did you find this out?" I asked her.

"I was in a shop," she explained as she opened her eyes and looked deep into mine. "You know I'm a big advocate of retail therapy."

I rolled my eyes and barely stifled a smile. "Don't I ever."

She smiled back then quickly turned serious again. "I was just wandering around the perfume section, spraying everything but not really smelling them," she started. Titania mimicked the motion of spraying perfume around herself. "And then I smelled something familiar and when I looked, I had sprayed myself with my sister's perfume."

Puck appeared out of thin air on the back of the couch. Fae sat there with faer legs crossed and munched on an apple. "And you didn't fall in love with the first schmuck you saw?" Fae asked.

"No!" A big grin formed across her face. "There was a retail worker who came up to me to ask if she could help me and...nothing."

I took a step back and examined Titania up and down. Gods, she was truly the most beautiful being in this entire dreadful existence of mine. "You're the cure."

Titania raised an eyebrow and scrunched her nose as I stared into her soul. "Huh?"

"You're immune to it because you're the cure to Love Sick," I further explained my point. "You hold the key to us figuring out how to ruin your sister's business. All we have to do is figure out how to extract it from you." I clapped my hands together and looked over at Puck. I mouthed 'find him,' to fae. With that, Puck poofed away.

"But why?" She asked with genuine confusion in her tone. "Why me? And how? I wasn't immune to the flower before."

"You were. I just never told you that you were." I sighed as the connection clicked for me. "When I created the flower, you were the only one I didn't want to trick. I wanted you to fall in love with me, for me."

"You created it?" She questioned as her brows rose and she blinked rapidly. "So that whole story about Cupid was a lie?"

"An exaggeration of the truth," I corrected. "Who do you think gave the seeds to Cupid?"

She rolled her eyes and mumbled, "Of fucking course." Titania chewed on her lip for a minute as she stared at the floor. When she looked back at me, she asked, "So why did it work with the... Will situation?"

I closed my eyes and inhaled deeply. I exhaled in a dramatic sigh. "He fell in love with you because of the flower," I explained to her. "Your feelings were genuine for him. Which is why I turned him into an ass."

She paused for a moment as she processed the new information. She had always been under the assumption that Love-in-idleness caused her feelings for Will, that's why she 'snapped' out of it when I turned Will into a donkey.

Truth be told, she fell out of love because she was blinded with rage at me. She felt like she could never truly be happy with me around. So she gave up after I turned him into a donkey and turned off her emotions for a few hundred years. When she left the kingdom, she turned them back on.

"So... what's next?" Titania inquired as she could finally formulate words after a few moments of silence.

"We need a mortal," I replied as I stroked my chin.

"Um...." Titania started, cocking her head to the side. "All of my court are faeries... And I don't want to bring any more of my family into this."

I bit my lip in thought. Chewing the skin off my lip, I held up a finger. "Did you bring the sample bottle?"

Titania searched through her purse before pulling out a miniature sized Love Sick bottle. "Oh, gods..." she trailed off as she held the bottle up and turned the label to face me. "I ran out of the store with it. Oh, dear."

"Okay." I took the bottle from her hand and examined it closer. "We need to spray someone in the hallway and make them fall in love with you."

"This sounds like a bad idea."

I laughed a hearty laugh, almost doubling over. "Aren't all my ideas bad ideas?"

"Well," Titania murmured, looking away from me and at the floor as she lowered her voice to below a whisper. "Not always."

I blinked a couple of times and turned my head to the side. It wasn't like Titania to give me compliments nowadays, even if it wasn't loud enough for a mouse to hear it from three feet away. Luckily, I had super senses and heard her just fine.

"Alright, fine." She looked back up at me. Her brows were drawn together and eyes determined. "How are we going to do this? You spray I follow?"

"Deal," I agreed.

Titania let out a long, exaggerated sigh and donned her disguise of a scarf and sunglasses once more. "Let's go."

With her permission, I took off in a jog to the door and flung it open. I looked both ways, hoping to see a bystander waiting to fall in love with a queen. My Queen. I ground my teeth at the empty halls. I took off down the hallway to the left, taking my next right, hurrying down a set of stairs, taking another right and then to the bottom floor where I walked out a glass door and into the pool area that was swarming with people. "Who wants to fall in love with a queen today?" I asked aloud.

"Oh gods," I heard Titania complain from behind me. "This is gonna make the news."

I looked around at all the people. The first man that caught my attention was a toned, oiled up, fine specimen of a man. He must have been an Athenian native with his tan skin and jet black hair. "Nope," I commented as he walked past us. "I don't think so. Next!"

"Do I get a say in this at all?" Titania called as she came up next to me.

I ignored her question as my attention was caught by an older man with dark leathery skin, wearing nothing but a blue speedo and an obnoxious gold chain that hung down. His shaggy salt and pepper hair and beard were drenched with chlorinated pool water. "Ah," I said as he got closer. "You'll do." As the man approached, I pulled out the sample bottle and began spraying him with it. He shut his eyes and began swatting the air before he turned around.

I ducked out of the way as the man opened his eyes to see Titania standing in front of him.

"You fucking asshole," Titania mumbled, chancing a glance at me.

I smiled at her and walked to the man. I put my arm around his shoulders before quickly removing it with a scrunched up nose. "You, sir, have earned a date with a queen."

"I swear to the gods, I will kill you," Titania growled at me. I winked at her and she scoffed, turning her attention back to the man. With a forced smile, she lowered her sunglasses and winked at the man. She blew a kiss for good measure. I was almost jealous. *Focus, Oberon.*

"'Ello beaut'," the Australian man purred as he presented her with a gap-toothed smile.

A nervous laugh emitted from Titania's lips. She forced a Russian accent as she said, "Privet."

I nonchalantly walked up to the pair, putting my arm around Titania and hovering my other above the wrinkly man's skin. "Ménage à trois, anyone?"

"This is a threesome, yes?" Titania sighed, sensing a trick up my sleeve that wasn't truly there.

"Sí," I confirmed, giving her what was supposed to be a 'trust me' smile.

"Wonderful," she grumbled, rolling her eyes.

"Back to our suite, then!"

The man reached down and grabbed Titania's ass, causing her to jump and flush. I grabbed his wrist and brought his hand to my ass. "Ah, ah, ah," I teased. "Can't have dessert before you have the appetizer, now can we?"

"Lead the way, my Queen," I said, swinging my arm out towards the door. "My new friend and I have a few things to bond over." I looked over at the panicked old man and smiled. "Isn't that right?" With wide eyes, he slowly nodded his head.

Without hesitation, Titania took off in a near jog to the door and back to our suite. I looked back at the old man and whispered to him. "You touch her only if I say and where I say, or I slice your penis from your body and shove it into your own ass."

We continued to follow Titania, the man staring at her the entire way back to our suite. Once we got to the room, I led the man by the hand to the bedroom. I smiled at him and pushed him down, straddling him.

I snapped my fingers and black tendrils of smoke wrapped around his eyes, wrists, and ankles. The man squirmed for a minute before settling down. "Wait here," I instructed to give him the illusion that he wasn't stuck there against his will.

I hurried out the door and almost knocked Titania down. "What the hell is the plan, Oberon?"

"You're going to spit in his face," I replied with a smirk.

"I'm not into degradation, darling." It was true. I had tried to get her to do it with me back in the day. Never did anything for her. "Giving or receiving."

"If he still loves you after you spit in his face, well, he's either still under the influence of Love Sick and saliva isn't the cure," I explained. I held back a laugh as I finished my statement. "Or he's into some really kinky shit, and saliva is the cure."

"So," Titania responded as she rolled her eyes. "We won't know either way? This seems like a terrible experiment."

"Oh, we'll know," I assured her. I put an arm around her and pulled her shoulder to shoulder with me.

"How?"

"Option B," I replied, looking over at her with a grin. "He asks you to do it again."

"Oh gods," Titania groaned. "There *is* a reason I turned down the dominatrix role."

I removed my arm and stepped away as I cocked my head to the side. "If your spit doesn't cure him, I don't know what will." I paused and stroked my goatee as I held up a finger. "Breast milk!"

"You're going down a dangerous path here, Oberon."

"Just go spit in the man's face," I shot back as I rolled my eyes and crossed my arms.

"Fine!" Titania swung the door open and marched to the blindfolded man. She hocked a big wad of saliva and spat it in the man's face.

The man screamed out in disgust and struggled in the restraints. He tried to get to his face to wipe the spit off as he sputtered.

I ran into the room upon hearing the man's screams. "I think it worked, Titania!"

"Oh gods," Titania whined as she rushed out of the room.

Hearing the footsteps of Titania hurrying out of the room, the man cried out, "Wait, my Queen, I forgive you!"

Titania stopped at the door and turned to look at me. "You were saying?"

I pressed my thumb into the center of my forehead and sighed. "Okay, your turn,"

"I am *not* peeing on him," she stated matter-of-factly.

I held up a finger again as the lightbulb went off. "I hadn't even considered that!"

"No! N. O. *No*!"

Ignoring her protests, I took off to the kitchen and returned with a clear plastic cup. "I have an idea!"

Titania rubbed her temples and murmured, "Faeries have all the magic in the world. Yet we still have to get migraines."

"Go pee in the cup," I commanded her as I extended the cup in her direction. "We'll make him drink it!"

"Absolutely not, Oberon!" She shouted, swiping my hand and the cup out of the air. "Even I have my limits." Titania closed her eyes and crossed her arms with a huff as she turned away from me.

"Titania!"

"NO!"

"For humanity!" I pleaded with her.

"I am *not* peeing for humanity," she grumbled, as she turned a menacing gaze towards me. "This is not two faeries, one cup."

I looked at her and back at the cup. With my free hand, I pointed my pointer finger at her. Then I pointed my pointer finger and extended my middle finger towards me. I held up the number two and the cup at the same time.

Trying not to laugh, Titania muttered, "We're just going to have to figure something else out, Oberon."

I ground my teeth. My body turned towards the wall and I let my head rest against it. I drew my fist back and punched the wall beside my head. The sheetrock exploded beneath the force of my fist. "I should know what the cure is," I ground out with tears welling up in my eyes.

"Okay, let's think about this logically," Titania murmured as she walked up and laid a gentle hand on my shoulder. "What else can be used to develop cures from a being? Cells! They made a vaccine because of the cells taken from Henrietta Lacks!"

"And just how do we collect your cells?" I asked as I turned my head towards her.

"You're the innovator," she reminded me as she took her hand off my back and crossed her arms. "Figure it out."

I pushed myself off the wall and took a blade out of my pocket. "Give me your hand," I said blankly.

She sighed and reluctantly gave me her hand. I gently slid the blade across her skin, pressing just hard enough to break the skin and draw blood. She scrunched her face as the blade slid across her skin.

"We'll knock out two birds with one stone. By cutting your hand with the blade, I'm collecting skin cells and blood cells," I explained to her. "Two different types of cells. One is bound to work."

I brought Titania's hand to my mouth and blew a breath of cold air across her wound. It healed as the air met the skin.

She stared at me wide eyed and whispered, "Thank you."

I nodded and turned to head back to the room. "I'm back, sweet cheeks," I purred as I entered. I grabbed his head and held it back. Prying open his mouth with one hand, I ran the bloody side of the blade across his tongue.

I snapped my fingers, and the tendrils of smoke around his eyes disappeared. He looked at me with the blade in my hand and his eyes went wide with fear.

Then, he looked past me and saw Titania. His face instantly relaxed as he said, "Hello, my Queen."

"Damn," Titania sighed. I ground my teeth as my nostrils flared. My grip on the knife tightened as I felt the wood handle begin to crack. "Spit won't work. Blood and skin cells don't work." She paused and started fanning herself as the emotions sank in. "Any other bright ideas?"

"I have one," I answered as I hung my head. "But you're not going to like it."

"Not. Peeing."

I shook my head. Knowing what I had to do, I took a deep breath and looked up at Titania. "How dare you leave me for a mortal, Titania? You threw everything away for a mere mortal who wound up deserting you in the end. The only man who ever loved you, despite your flaws, was the one you threw aside."

Wide eyed and blinking rapidly, Titania took a step back at my seemingly sudden and suspicious outburst. "Excuse me? This is neither the time nor the place."

"It's as good a time as any," I spat with as much venom as I could muster. I shut my eyes to hold back the tears I was fighting. Truly, I didn't want to do this to her, but I knew I had to try. "You left me and everything we had behind. Had you not done that, we wouldn't be in this situation!"

"Don't you *dare* blame this on me," she shot back. "*You* are the one who played too many games in our marriage!"

"Oh, I was the only one who played games, Titania?" I questioned, almost hurt. "Need I remind you of Will? What about your affair with the married Irish king, Finvarra?"

"We both had extramarital affairs, that's true," she reluctantly admitted. "But you were the one who manipulated with your magic! You made these flowers! You said so yourself! If you'd never made those wretched things, this never would have happened! And you have the audacity to blame *me*?"

"Because it *is* your fault, Tati! You're too self-centered and entitled to see that!" I shouted without thinking. I stopped myself before I could say anything else hurtful.

"You really did it this time."

Tears began streaming down her cheeks. "Fix this yourself," she spat and turned around. "I'm going home."

"Always running from your problems, and never facing them!"

"Fuck you, you old fool!" She shouted as she stormed out of the suite.

I followed after her with a cup and held it to Titania's cheek. She pushed me away from her and swatted her hands at me. "Get off of me!"

"Just hold still!"

"*No!*" She screamed as she backed away. "Get off of me! Let me go!"

"Tears, Titania," I explained as I held up the cup.

"What?" She asked between sniffles.

"What *didn't* we try?" She put her hands down and walked towards me and the cup in my hand. I held it up to her face, and she didn't push me away. The tears flowed freely and into the cup as she cried at the wound in her heart that my words had caused. "I'm sorry. They had to be real tears. Fake tears never would have worked."

She stayed silent and looked away from me. I took her hand in my free one. "I didn't mean any of it, Titania," I promised her.

She pulled her hand away and wiped her tears. "Just go see if it works."

A camera shutter sounded behind me. I spun around to see Bradley dashing around the corner. *Sonuvabitch.* Where was Puck? Why hadn't fae alerted me that Bradley was here? *If you want something done right, you have to do it yourself.*

I gritted my teeth and looked at the direction Bradley had taken off down and back at the open suite of the door. I had a decision to make, and Bradley wasn't worth the extra headache right then. Plus, there was no way I could leave Titania after what had just happened.

I ran into the suite and poured the tears into the man's mouth. The man looked at me and questioned, "Where is my Queen?"

I slammed my fist onto the nightstand, crumpling its legs and cracking its top. "Godsdammit!" I shouted. I looked into the mirror across the room and saw my black pupils had encompassed the entirety of my eyes. Out in the hallway, I could hear Titania still crying.

Puck appeared out of thin air. "I can't find him," they said with disappointment and fear riddled in faer voice.

"Did you check the hotel, Puck?" I turned to face fae.

"No..." Fae admitted and shrank back, fearing retribution for failing me.

"He was here," I informed fae. "I don't think Titania saw who it was, but she knows someone has a picture of us now."

"I'm guessing the tests didn't go well?" Puck asked with a nod towards the man. Fae was a little more confident after I hadn't freaked the fuck out on them.

I shook my head and looked down. The front door closed followed by the sound of the shower running. I looked over at Puck. "If she asks, I've gone to bed."

"Where are you going?"

"I'm going to handle this Bradley situation. Once and for all."

"Oberon, you have that look in your eyes."

I shook my head. "I have to do this, Puck, for her."

"Is that what this is about?" Puck countered. "You're doing this to get her back and not to save humanity?"

That was my breaking point. I slammed my forearm into faer neck and pushed fae against the wall. I got in close to faer ears, my lips brushing against them. "You don't question me. Understood?"

"Mmmhmm," Puck managed.

I let fae go and fae dropped to the ground, clutching faer neck. Puck was gasping for air as fae grabbed the edge of the dresser and stood up. I tossed faer a set of keys and fae grabbed them out of the air. "Give those to her when she wakes up in the morning. I'll send her the coordinates to give to the pilot."

"Oberon..." Puck began. I shot faer a 'choose your next words wisely' look. "Don't go back to your old self, please."

"Failure."

"Killer."

"Murderer."

My migraine stayed with me into the night and was still lingering when my tired eyes cracked open to the morning light. The pastry box lay open next to me on the bed, reminding me that the pastries and sweets I had bought for all three of us had become my comfort meal the night before. Judging from how swollen my eyes still were, they didn't help much.

A loud ding drew my attention to my phone, which had been hastily thrown onto the bedside table. Three missed calls. One was from my agent, one was from Chad, and one was from Amira. There were also about twenty texts from those three as well as my glam team. Something was very wrong.

Tapping on the news articles in the texts revealed the candid photo that was taken of me and Oberon in the hotel hallway the night before. Without the context of our true story, the angle of the photo suggested a public display of affection. Passion so out of control that Oberon had pinned me up against the wall before we could get to our room. And of course, the headline chose to push that incorrect narrative.

"Fuck!" I flew out of my hotel bed, throwing on one of the hotel's complimentary robes to cover my naked form. "Oberon!" I ran out of the separate bedroom to the double doors of Oberon's room. I started pounding on the door, aiming to wake him if he wasn't already up. Or rather still awake.

"No, Your Majesty," Puck said, appearing beside me and leaning against the other door. "Not here, my Queen. His Majesty knows and I won't have you two killing each other right now."

"Where the hell is he?"

Puck shrugged. "He went for a walk. Didn't say where he was going."

I huffed out a breath. "If he's not here, can you at least let me in?" I didn't really know why I wanted to be in Oberon's room. I just know that I didn't want to be alone in mine.

Before I could receive an answer, my phone dinged again. Another text. *Oh, god. What now?* I was relieved a bit when I saw it was from Oberon and not from a member of my team or family. It was just one of his terribly confusing texts that only held coordinates.

"Belay that order," I said, waving Puck off. I plugged the coordinates into my phone as I rushed back to my room to get dressed.

"Tati!" Puck called to me, chasing me back to my room.

As I rushed around my room, getting dressed in the most comfortable and inconspicuous outfit I had packed, I caught a glimpse of the hotel's street entrance through the window. There was a mob of people hanging outside the door, and more people curiously joined the fray with each passing moment. "I need you to get me out of here unseen," I told Puck without looking at faer.

The sound of keys jingling on my bed pulled my attention. "He said to give you these if you rushed off."

I picked up the keyset, not recognizing them. "What are these for?"

"Go to the rooftop?"

The rooftop? What Mission Impossible exit strategy did he expect me to come up with? I stared at my phone, finding where the coordinates were pointing me to. "What is he planning?"

"My Queen," Puck answered the rhetorical question I asked to the general vicinity. "I can honestly say I have no idea."

A new text from Oberon came in, showing the emoji with the quirked eyebrow. With a sigh, I texted '**OMW**' in response.

Fixing my sunglasses on my face, I sighed and peeked out into the hallway. The coast was clear. In fact, it felt like there wasn't another guest anywhere on this penthouse floor. The hotel must have upped the security in the time since the incriminating photo of me and Oberon was released. It was definitely possible that Oberon threatened them into doing so, but I was relieved all the same.

I stealthily made my way to the stairwell at the corner of the building. "My Queen?" I heard once I was safe behind the heavy door.

"Yes, Robin?"

"He was very unstable when he left. Be careful." I could hear the concern in Puck's voice, and that serious tone was enough to get anyone's attention if they knew Puck well. Fae were always the most jovial of company, finding jokes and laughs in even the most dire of circumstances. When Puck would get serious, it would make both the seelie and unseelie courts worry. And I was no different. But before I could respond, fae disappeared in a cloud of smoke.

The word of warning made me hesitate in the stairwell. *Maybe I shouldn't go.*

But what else can I do?

Go home.

To a daughter who is still hypnotized into loving my fiancé and a family that is going to have far too many questions about the tabloids. And I will have no explanation that would please everyone. My life and my family as I know it will be over.

That thought was enough to get my feet moving again. I darted up the last flight of stairs until I came to a heavy industrial door that was locked. Fumbling with the key set, I managed to unlock and throw open the door.

The helicopter that was waiting for me chopped the air around me, messing my hair and clothes. There was a pilot in the copter, waiting for me. "Oberon, what did you do?"

"Look what you've done now."

"You've really gone and fucked everything up now."
"You really think she is going to forgive you after this?"
"Murderer."

"SILENCE!" I threw a bolt of energy from my palm into the side of the wall of the abandoned castle. The bolt struck the wall and shook the castle. Debris fell from the wall and the roof, one rock nearly smacking me in the head. Heavy, deep breaths escaped the shallow slit between my lips. I turned around to face the man I had taken captive and brought to this remote island.

"Bradley, Bradley, Bradley," I started as I stepped towards him. "Tsk, tsk, tsk." I put a finger under his chin and his eyes nearly bulged out of his head. He lifted his head with the pressure of my finger digging into the underside of his jaw. His breathing hitched as his gaze met mine.

Bradley attempted to mumble something that sounded a bit like 'Yumsumbish'.

I laughed at his pathetic attempt to squirm and try to untie his hands. Once he gave up the squirming, I pulled the gag that was in his mouth out and let it fall to his chest. "You were saying?"

"You son of a bitch!" He shouted as he tried to lunge forward. With his lunge came his downfall as the chair tipped over and Bradley landed face first on the cobblestone floor.

Laughing again, I reared my foot back and kicked him in the ribs, sending him tumbling over. Still tied to the chair, Bradley made more jerky movements to try to break the magic bound around his wrists and ankles.

"There he is."

"There is the Oberon we all know."

"Kill him, Oberon."

"Kill him."

"Kill him."

"Kill him!"

Closing my eyes to block out the voices, I grabbed Bradley by his almond brown shaggy hair and lifted him off the ground, bringing his face to mine. I cocked my head to the side as I stared into his gray eyes. "Shall we try this again?"

"What do you want from me?" He turned his tactic from being a prick to trying to reason with me.

"I want to know who sent you." I dropped him to the ground while the chair legs caught him from falling all the way to the ground.

"Sent me where?"

I raised my hand and brought the back across his cheek. "To follow me!"

Blood spilled from between his lips as he spit out a couple of teeth. "Following you?" He laughed. "I don't even *know* you!"

"Then why were you taking pictures of me?" I snapped. My fingers curled around his throat, crushing his windpipe. His eyes bulged out of his head and he did everything he could do to squirm loose from my grip. Once nothing worked to loosen my grip, he let his body go limp and dropped his chin against my hand.

"I wasn't taking pictures of you," he admitted, voice strained. "I was following Tati Hastings."

My heart dropped but at the same time, my blood boiled. I was furious, confused, and hurt. Why would he be following Titania around like that? He was her ex-husband and had no claim to her. He didn't have any right to be following her and taking pictures of her.

"What makes you any different?"

"Didn't you follow her around for a century before you finally decided to live your own life?"

"Hypocrite."

"Accept it, you aren't special."

My eyes went wide, and I scrunched up my nose. I felt my grip around Bradley's throat tightening slightly as my breathing quickened. I stared through Bradley and at the wall behind him while my fingers continued their crushing crusade. I heard Bradley gurgling through the sound of my teeth grinding together.

His eyes slowly fluttered shut. I released my grip and shoved him backwards, tipping his chair and causing him to fall on his back. Turning around, I made my way to the opposite side of the room. My hand covered my mouth and ran down along my goatee.

Frustrated, I slammed my fist into the wall. I felt my knuckles connect with the stone, leaving an imprint of my fist in the stone wall. The wall shook, and I pressed my forehead against the rough, cool stone wall. I turned around and walked back towards Bradley, still laying on his back but he'd given up on fighting for now.

"Why were you taking pictures of her?" I asked, standing over his battered and bruised body.

"To get back at the bitch," he spat, his voice gravelly from the damage his throat had taken. The spittle flew up and came right back down on his face. He shook his head to try to get it off of him, but to no avail. I put pressure on his shoulder. He squirmed but grinned and bore it.

"Let's try that again, and perhaps we won't speak of the lady like that again. Why were you taking pictures of her?"

"She left me and I wanted to get back at her."

"Back at her, how?" I snapped, pressing my heel deeper into his shoulder.

"I... I didn't know," he confessed as a tear slipped out of his eye. "I just wanted to find her doing something she shouldn't have been."

I removed my foot from his shoulder and stepped to the side. "Why?"

"To ruin her life and career." I noticed him rolling his shoulder to try and relieve the pain I had caused. "The bitch deserved it." I lifted my foot and stomped on his shoulder. The audible cracking of his bones echoed throughout the throne room.

"Kill him, Oberon."

"Don't wait for her to get here."

"She'll stop you."

"Kill him!"

The sound of helicopter propellers spinning in the ocean sky traveled down the corridors of the castle. Once I heard the *whooshing* of the helicopter get closer, I grabbed Bradley by the hair and lifted him up. Sitting him back on all four legs of the chair, I smiled and pulled out the sample bottle of Love Sick.

"It's showtime."

C her really thought turning back time was a good thing? I couldn't help but think that to myself as a far too familiar sight came into view. That tiny island off the coast of France held what was our secret romantic getaway location; a castle of dark stone and icy light. I never knew whether Oberon traded for it, built it, or simply took ownership of a pre-existing structure. I honestly didn't bother to ask. All I needed to know was that he came into possession of it as a gift to me. To give us a vacation home when we were still married, still in love, and taking a break from the rest of the world.

It was easy to hide from the mortal world. A simple spell made it visible only from the air, and very few, if any, flights ever took a route that would reveal it. If any flights went over it, none of the passengers were ever paying enough attention to see it. If they were paying close enough attention and caught a glimpse, they either didn't speak or weren't believed. Whatever the case, maybe, it was clear that it was still untouched by mortals.

When was the last time we came here together? It must've been towards the end of our marriage. Oberon would have brought me here the moment he sensed I was cross with him to seduce or love bomb me into staying. *Let's see it would have been... the day after William's funeral.*

Oh, that day was a terrible mess. I was a complete wreck, mourning a former lover. His brilliance was already being called into question by people like that arrogant blowhard Robert Greene. How dare he attempt to destroy the Bard's impeccable image and claim he was too uneducated to write his plays? He was that green-eyed monster Will once wrote of, incensed that his vast generational wealth and a bought degree from Oxford didn't make him a genius. Meanwhile, my playwright of meager means and education wrote almost thirty plays that are still remembered for their wisdom, their wit, and their stories. And those thirty-six plays were just the tip of the iceberg known as his genius. If given immortality, William could have written a thousand more, and all of them would be better than even the top scripts I was being handed in the modern day.

The day he died, I not only mourned him, I mourned the stories he would never get to tell.

I had tried so hard to make it happen. I submitted a petition to allow him to be made immortal with the seelie, like me and my court. I made the absolute best arguments I could.

And the one person who stood in my way was my husband. Oberon.

After William had died, Oberon knew I was deep in mourning for the man. And he knew the moment I had moved from the denial phase into the anger phase, he was going to be my target. He tried to mitigate and pacify my rage in advance by dragging me to this, our vacation home, and caring for me.

It didn't help him or me.

The helicopter landed, and I stepped out, taking in the sight. Oberon had clearly been here since our separation; it was obvious in how he had repaired the path of destruction I had left when I walked out of his life and our marriage. So many mixed emotions stirred within me, but the predominant one was worry. Our presence here didn't bode well.

As I walked through the castle, I could hear Oberon cackling. The sound grew louder and louder with every step towards the throne room. When I reached the throne room, I found my ex-husband draped sideways across his throne, laughing at nothing but himself and whatever the voices in his head were saying.

Despite my delicate steps, Oberon sensed my presence and immediately stopped laughing, snapping himself to an upright position. A futile attempt to hide his breaking sanity. "Oberon?" I asked cautiously.

"Yes, my love?" From the shadows of the dark castle came murmurs and shuffling. There was something dark here. And it was preying on Oberon.

"What's going on?"

"Do you not remember this place?" The shadows murmured again, not echoing Oberon's words, but they weren't clear enough for me to tell what they were truly saying. Knowing Oberon, they weren't words of kindness.

"No, I do... But why are we here?"

With a snap of his fingers, the shadows started dragging a human form out in front of me. They were dressed in modern clothes that had rips, scuffs, and stains from a brawl. Their head was covered with a bag, maybe a pillowcase, and their hands were tied behind their back. "I found the rat."

I furrowed my brows as I looked up at Oberon. "What rat?"

"The one that leaked the photo to the press."

Oh, Gods. "And you kidnapped him?!"

"Kidnapped is a strong word." Oberon's prisoner jolted, letting out a muffled insult. They were gagged beneath the bag, too. "I didn't hurt him. Much. Just a little Love Sick to make him fall in love with me."

I rubbed my temples, feeling my migraine make a stronger comeback than Robert Downey Jr. *We're going to have to unpack that sometime soon.* "Oberon, have you ever heard of something called a 'lawsuit'?"

Oberon shrugged, trying so hard to hide his smug, Joker-like grin. Every time I saw that smile, I became more and more convinced that Nicholson absolutely took inspiration for the character from Oberon, whether he realized it or not. "Love makes people do stupid things."

"And what exactly does this solve?"

Rather than answering me outright himself, Oberon nodded towards the hooded figure. "Take a peek at who it is."

Again, my brows furrowed with confusion. Oberon would not have done this and told me to look at who the stalker was if it didn't matter. And the fact that it did matter was concerning. I reached up, took a corner of the pillowcase and gently slid it off the prisoner's head.

Bradley's bruised and cut face glared up at me from beneath a mussed mop of brown curls. "You..." was all I could say as my heart stopped for a moment.

"He followed us, Titania. All the way to Greece. He was the one in the hallway. He sold the pictures to the media."

That was all I needed to hear. Using my index finger, I yanked the gag out of Bradley's mouth, pulling it down over his chin and letting it fall around his neck. "How long have you been doing this? Following me around, snapping pictures for you to twist?"

Bradley's cracked lips twisted into a devilish smile. A smile I once thought merely hid an impish sense of humor. Not a hunger for petty revenge. "Months. I knew you'd slip up, Tati. You always do."

"Do you have any idea what you've done?" I asked rhetorically, raising my voice. "I am not the only victim of your revenge porn here. Do you have any idea how you've humiliated our daughters?" *Oh, gods. The girls. If he's been here the whole time. They're having to go through all of this with nothing but body guards to help them through it. I'll never forgive him for that.*

Bradley shrugged. "Whatever it took to take you down. To show them how you're not the magical being you portray yourself to be. That you aren't unstoppable. That even the mighty eventually fall."

"Magical? Mighty? Oh, darling," I purred out with an edge of menace to my voice. I could feel the electricity tingling between my fingers before I conjured the lightning in my hand, twisted into a well-manicured claw. "You don't even know the half of it."

Rather than being shocked like most mortals would be to seeing the impossible, Bradley barked out a laugh. "You think I haven't caught on to your magic? There were things that just didn't make sense about our marriage." Okay, so I might have used a little magic to streamline the necessary parts of my life. It wasn't exactly easy to be the perfect mother and a movie star. So yes, I used my magic to maintain the balance. Maybe to also get more parts than I normally would have by myself alone. And sometimes I made myself correct during a domestic tiff or two. "But when I started following you and seeing your mystical boyfriend over here use magic, I put it together."

I heard Oberon grunt through his teeth, but cut him off before he could go any further. "Darling," I purred with that edge of menace again. "You are speaking to the parents of the Earth. The weather goes completely to shit when we're unhappy. Why do you think California has been in a drought since the dawn of time? Are you really stupid enough to piss me off *deliberately*?"

Bradley's smug facade cracked a bit as he winced. Yet he tried to cover it up by saying, "You're done for, Tati."

Lightning continued to crackle in my hands, and distant thunder rumbled. "I am as old as the world itself. I have survived countless wars, plagues, famines, and brought down men far more powerful than you over thousands of years. You're the one that's finished, Bradley." I forced the pillow case back over his head and took a step back. The lightning in my hands gave way to water. Waterboarding wasn't usually my preferred method of karma, but I had the opportunity. And I was going to take it.

"*Enough!*" Oberon's call to order was louder than the thunder that I had conjured with my fury.

"Stay out of this, Oberon." I kept my voice even and authoritative, showing that I would not be intimidated into backing down.

"I won't let you do something you'll regret, Titania," he said, stepping down from his throne.

"Then why bring him to me?"

"I didn't. I brought you to me."

I rolled my eyes, still spinning the water between my hands. "Semantics."

"I can handle the mortal. It was you who needed to see what he did. Not him who needed to be punished by you. The mortals aren't like us, Titania." *Brilliant deduction, Sherlock.* "They aren't capable of love like we are. Not anymore, at least. Humanity lost their love and compassion because we lost ours for one another."

I scoffed. "I would *love* to see how you came to that conclusion." I made the mistake of taking a look over at Oberon. I was greeted with him looking at me from over his dark, round sunglasses. "What?"

"What did you just say, Titania?"

I said I would love—Fuck. "I would very much like to see how you came to that conclusion."

"Do you think our reach extends only to the weather?" Oberon asked, ignoring my attempt to cover up my previous statements. "You think the weather is the only force on this planet that changes when we change? Human emotions change when the very beings that gave them those emotions change. The world changes with us, because of us. We fell out of love and the love left the world. Why would it stay when the creators of sanctimony no longer believed in the matrimony that brought them together?"

"Are we really doing this right now?" I asked flatly.

Bradley turned his covered head toward Oberon, following his voice. "My love, can you please remove this bag from my head?" *And suddenly, I am realizing my worst nightmare: my exes getting together.*

"Oh, fuck off." With a snap of Oberon's fingers, Bradley's body twisted, strained, and stretched. The bag on his head and the binds that kept his hands behind his back ripped apart as his flesh grew gray hair. His ears, mouth, and nose elongated as his hands and feet morphed into hooves.

Finally, my jackass ex-husband... was a literal jackass.

Which made my worst nightmare even worse as he trotted up to Oberon and started nuzzling him. If it were any other circumstance, it would almost look cute. Instead, it was a dark reminder of the bigger problem we faced.

"Okay, we have to find a cure for Love Sick," Oberon said, echoing my thoughts. "I can't have a donkey trying to bone me for eternity."

I suppressed the shiver that wanted to roll through my body and replied, "I might actually be willing to pee on this one." Donkey Bradley brayed loudly, clearly protesting the idea of receiving a golden shower from me. "Play stupid games, win stupid prizes, jackass."

"Titania," Oberon called with great seriousness, signaling a change of subject. "You have to see how important our love is to the world."

"I swear to the gods, if you start singing."

Oberon sighed at my jest and stepped closer to me. "Titania, listen to what I'm saying. I love you."

Always walking away from the problem and never facing them! Was it my mind that was playing those echoing words from my most recent memory? Or was it the haunted nature of our old vacation home's halls? "Your words yesterday suggest otherwise."

"I told you why I had to say those things. It was the only way to make sure they were real tears!"

"You never lie, Oberon."

My words made the King of the Faeries hang his head. "I never said I wasn't lying." *I knew it.* "Yes, I felt all those things at *one point*. I felt them when you first left me. I felt it when you told me to fuck off at the restaurant. Okay? I felt it. Then I realized I was wrong. I wasn't talking to you when I said you were too self-centered to see it was your fault. I was looking into my own eyes in the mirror behind you. That's the only way I was able to say that and not burst into flames." *He was saying all of that to himself? Is this how he always talks to himself?* "When I said them, though, I didn't believe them."

"No one ever says things they don't mean. Not when they're that angry." I certainly wasn't capable of lying when I was enraged like that. Rage made me the most honest version of myself. That's why I had to keep it under control. Because the damage would be far too great. And it wasn't the damage to my career that I was worried about. It was the damage I could do to others that scared me the most.

"As I said, I meant that at one point."

"You should mean them now. He certainly would agree with you," I said, nodding to Bradley the Donkey.

"I can't mean them. The truth is all of this is my fault. If I hadn't created the damned flower, we wouldn't be here. If I hadn't made the flowers go extinct, we wouldn't be here. If I hadn't been such a condescending, narcissistic asshole during our entire marriage, we wouldn't be here. And if I hadn't tried to make you fall in love with me, we wouldn't be here."

It was my turn to hang my head as I heard my first ex-husband take on too much of the blame and responsibility. "You're hardly solely to blame. I was terribly self-centered. Still am, according to the ass. Petty. I tend to hold a grudge."

Oberon turned away from me. "The truth is, Titania, I stopped blaming you for leaving me a long time ago. I decided I would never be with another man or woman until I could become the man you deserve to be with. And I'm trying. The darkness that lived within me will always be a part of me.

"That's why I brought you here. I love you, Titania, and I want you to love me back again. But you're going to have to accept this." Oberon opened his arms wide, gesturing to the cold castle that surrounded us. "This darkness that resides in me will always be here. What I wanted to truly show you, though, was that I've changed. The Oberon of old would have killed the rat like the snake he was. But that's not me anymore. I want to be better. For you and with you."

I looked around at the cold castle, finally knowing how he came into possession of it all these centuries later. He made this. This place that was our home on occasion was made of the poison that was born into his mind. I genuinely never would have guessed; not by how it looked and not by how Oberon and I treated it. This was a sanctuary. A safe place for us to hide from the world. And even each other when things got bad. Oberon took the darkness inside of him, used it to create this getaway for me. And he forced himself to join me even as he was surrounded by the living embodiment of his mental illnesses. He forced himself to be a literal prisoner in his mind... for me.

My feet took control, leading me to step up to Oberon. My eyes pierced through the darkness of his lenses to find the irises of his eyes. He looked back at me for a moment before raising his hand to gently cup my face. His forehead naturally inclined down to lean against mine. We had not touched one another like this in centuries. And despite the cold darkness that built this keep of his, his touch was warm and gentle against my skin. I raised my hand to touch the hand that held my face, feeling the callouses of endless hard work that had grown over the years.

"I'm sorry, Titania. For all the ways I've ever hurt you."

The gentle words drew tears to my eyes that rolled down my cheeks and tumbled to the floor. Those tears were quickly licked up by Bradley the Donkey, who had been nibbling on Oberon's sports jacket for attention.

Out of nowhere, Bradley brayed and charged between us, pushing us apart and knocking Oberon back towards his throne. "You ass," Oberon growled.

"What's gotten into him?" I asked

Right as Oberon was getting his feet back under him, Bradley let loose and kicked his hind legs right into Oberon's stomach, sending him back down to the floor. "This is an awfully weird way to show me love, Bradley."

As Bradley continued to bray at Oberon, I thought back to what the end of our marriage was like. Yes, I was petty, self-centered, and a pain in the ass. But Bradley would get violent. I knew the precise day that he fell out of love with me because it was the first time he ever tried to strike me. I called the divorce lawyer the next day while Bradley spent the evening in a jail cell. "He is not in love."

"He has to be," Oberon protested, waving his hand to freeze Bradley while in mid-bucking position. "Love Sick doesn't just stop working."

I brushed my fingertips against my cheek, feeling the wet trail my tears had left behind. "It does if the target is hit with the antidote."

"What antidote?"

"Our antidote. He ate my tears that I cried just now."

"But tears don't work. Remember?"

That's right. They didn't work the day before. So why would they work now? What was different? "... Hurt and angry tears didn't work. But these tears did."

Oberon's furrowed brows relaxed as he followed my train of thought. "Happy tears. Tears of love." I nodded at him. "You know what this means?"

"We have a cure!"

"And a coverup for why we're together in Greece."

Oh. Right. The tabloids. The Paparazzi. My family. They all still thought I was cheating on Chad and sneaking around behind everyone's back. "Come back to that later," I said, not wanting to think about that stressful situation and just wanting to exist in the relief that I knew how to save my daughter.

"They go hand-in-hand," Oberon pointed out. "We have the cure. Now we have to make perfume and cologne. We were together as business partners."

It could work. And if anyone asked why I didn't tell them, I could just say Oberon had a strict NDA that prohibited me from saying a word. They knew I took contracts seriously. "Then what are we waiting for?"

We returned to the hotel via helicopter to avoid the swarm of paparazzi that had formed around the building. They looked like tiny ants scouring for tidbits of leftover food to feed their almighty Queen. Little did they know, they were pissing off a colony of fire ants. If they didn't disperse before too long, I would unleash a thunderstorm never before seen by the people of Greece.

Once I had collected a few of Titania's happy tears and put her to bed, I went to work on the formula for the cure. I finally had the final bit, but I just needed to find a way to mass produce Titania's happy tears. Mimicking the salinity in water to essentially form the same liquid as a tear was easy if one was trying to mimic human tears, but magical tears were a different beast altogether. Unlike humankind, our body was made up of sixty percent magic as opposed to human's sixty percent water. Replicating magic was much harder than replicating water.

Luckily for a mad magic scientist like me, I had replicated magic tears before. Using a bit of my own blood, I was able to extract the magic from the blood cells. Once that was done, I would need to find a way to replicate Titania's reminiscence in the artificial tears. I stroked my goatee and leaned back in my chair. Chewing on my lip, I pondered just how I could recreate Titania's magic fingerprint.

"Something so simple."

"Yet so far out of reach."

"Yearn for the answer."

"As the pot, we stir."

"Your mind we breach."

"Watch as you dwindle."

I closed my eyes and snapped my fingers to turn up the music. I fought the words thrown around in my mind. The anger and disappointment in myself for feeling so lost and hopeless when it came to what should have been such an easy answer. The beating of the music drowned out my thoughts as I tapped my foot to the beat. I took the pencil from behind my ear and tapped it against the top of the desk I had been hunched over for the better part of the night.

As my fingers twitched with the music and my foot tapped to the beat, I felt myself drift off into a state of euphoria. Suddenly I felt weightless, floating through the clouds and being cooled by the water particle that formed the white cotton balls that floated with me through my euphoric state of mind. With every beat drop of the music, I felt myself plummeting towards the earth like I was on a roller coaster. The drop was exhilarating every time, and the climb relaxed the muscles that may have gotten sore from the drop.

"Oberon," a voice called.

My eyes remained closed as I floated, not wanting to let go of the momentary solitude I had built in my mind. That feeling of floating, of being dropped and picked back up, was exhilarating and made all of my nerves tingle with anticipation.

"Oberon."

I ignored the voice as it echoed in my mind. My mind floated through the confines of every neuron and electrode that made up my brain. I was at peace, floating amongst myself and my own thoughts. It was the most at peace I had been since... Titania.

"Oberon," I heard her call again. I opened my eyes to see Titania standing over me with two cups of coffee. She half smiled at me as my eyes fluttered open. "I thought you might need a cup of coffee after working all night, but," she paused and wiped the corner of my lip. "It appears you got some sleep after all."

I chuckled and took the cup of coffee from her. "Yes, I suppose so." I took a sip from the coffee and immediately my eyes grew wide with delight, my eyebrows bounced up towards my hairline, and a smile crept across my face. "Irish coffee, I see."

"No other way to make coffee, if you ask me." Titania smiled back as she took a sip of her Irish coffee. "Did you get it figured out?"

I arched an eyebrow as I sipped my coffee. "Come again?"

"The cure," Titania clarified. "Did you figure it out?"

I sighed and shook my head. "I'm stuck."

Titania looked at me with an arched brow. "The great mastermind, Oberon, stumped after all these years."

I rolled my eyes and turned my head so she wouldn't see the smile I was hiding from her. "It feels like the answer is right in front of my eyes, but I just can't place it." I laid my coffee cup down on the desk.

"Maybe I can be of some help?" She offered as she sat her coffee cup down on the desk next to mine.

"I'm just having trouble remembering how to copy a magic fingerprint," I confessed. "It is something I have done a hundred times before, but for some reason, I simply can't put my finger on what I need to do."

"Why do you need to copy a magic fingerprint for the cure? You have a vial of my tears."

"If we're going to mass produce this, we're going to have to figure out a formula. We can't just expect you to sit in a factory like a dairy cow being drained of your tears," I explained to her. "I have the magic essence. I just need your magic fingerprint to add to it."

"Can you do it in a similar manner to how humans replicate DNA?"

"You mean taking some of your saliva and extracting the fingerprint? But how does that help me mass produce it?" I questioned as I cocked my head to the side.

"Like they do, causing a reaction within the fingerprint that forces it to replicate."

My mouth dropped at the extent of Titania's knowledge of the human DNA reproduction cycle. "So split the double helix to force it to begin the reproduction process?"

"Train it for a few hours to continually repeat," she explained. "Then it will continue to replicate itself and you'll be able to use it continuously to build the cure."

My jaw hit the floor as I leaned forward with my elbows propped up in my lap. "How in the world do you know this?"

"I played a scientist who was practicing cloning once in a movie," she explained. "And you, of all people, darling, should know that I go all in for every role."

I jumped up and kissed Titania's forehead. "Thank you, Titania. You have once again saved the day."

She laughed, half out of shock from the kiss on the forehead and half from the shock of me giving her such a dramatic compliment. I grabbed both coffee cups and drained them back to back into my mouth. With a new jolt of energy, I kicked Titania out of the room and locked the door behind her. It was time to do mad scientist shit.

22
Tati

I turned my phone in my hand over and over again, trying to work up the courage to make the call. I had been on the world's stages and screens. I'd attended a number of award shows, and I lived with the paparazzi following my every move. And none of that could prepare me for how nervous I was to call my family after everything that had transpired in the last forty-eight hours.

I'd gone over the lie in my head a million times, and it would certainly be easier to lie over the phone where they could only hear my voice and not see my face or body language. But still, I never liked lying to my loved ones unless I absolutely had to.

I knew that I needed to get this done sooner rather than later. The longer it took for me to call and explain, the angrier everyone was going to be. I'd already put it off for too long trying to come up with something to say that wouldn't demolish the foundation I had set.

Was that even possible at this point? We were in a fragile state before this all began.

Who should I even call first? Malika wouldn't pick up if she was still under my sister's spell and hated my guts. Sami was still just a little girl, and even though she most likely had questions, I didn't want to grow her up too fast. So that left Amira, mature beyond her years but still just a child who had been unfairly forced to play the mediator between me and the others during my trip. And Chad, the person who would have the most questions and who I was the most afraid of talking to at this point.

Men would come and go, but I always needed to be there for my children. I pulled Amira's phone number up and hit 'dial'.

My heart was pounding with each ring. I briefly considered that maybe it would be better if Amira didn't answer and if I was sent to voicemail. But that would just postpone the conversation, and it needed to happen before the circumstances got any worse.

"Mom?" The one word broke my heart, lifted my spirits, and put the fear of all the gods into me.

"Hello, darling. How are you?"

"Well, if I'm honest, Mom, I'm a little pissed." I winced. Even though colorful language was common and even appropriate for people of her age, Amira very rarely cursed herself. She only did it when all other words failed to effectively communicate her message and intentions.

"I don't blame you one bit, darling."

"Are you really cheating on Chad?"

"Of course, I'm not, darling. You know how the paparazzi like to twist even the most innocent things into something they're not."

"Mom." Amira's tone fell to that tone I would take when I didn't want my children to lie to my face. "I saw the picture. Obe was literally pinning you to the wall."

"Yes, but not because we were… doing that." I had given my girls 'the talk' years ago, and I certainly wasn't naïve enough to think that a teenager on the verge of adulthood wasn't more aware of sex and what it entailed. Still, I felt the need to somewhat censor myself. Probably due to discomfort.

"Then what were you two doing? How do you even know him? I thought you said cryptocurrency was just a scam."

"And I still do. This has nothing to do with his cryptocurrency company."

"Then what does it have to do with?"

I sighed. "You know that Obe is a prolific entrepreneur. He likes to dabble in new industries and try new things."

"Yeah. So?"

"Well, he's working on creating a fragrance company, and he wanted me to be the model and spokesperson for his... perfume magnum opus, for lack of a better way to put it. We've been discussing the logistics and everything for months, and we're in Greece right now because we're shooting the launch commercial and doing a photo shoot for the PR packages." It wasn't a complete lie.

"So, what's with the photo?"

"Darling, what you can't see in that photo is that I'm crying. When we originally planned this shoot, everything was going well at home. And then, just a few days before I flew out, your sister started acting out. I tried to convince Obe to change the shoot date, but everything was already booked and I'd signed a contract saying that I'd be here during this time. If I didn't come, I'd be in breach of contract and Obe could have sued me."

"So you still went, so that you didn't lose money."

"No! Darling, I still went because the last thing our family needs is another soap opera to add drama to our lives. I didn't want to put you all through the hullabaloo of a court case. You saw what happened with the Johnny Depp/Amber Heard trial. Can you imagine throwing that brand of chaos on top of everything else? You girls have been through so much already this year. I didn't want to make it worse."

There was a pause on Amira's end, indicating that she was allowing my words to sink in before she responded. "This still doesn't explain the photo."

"We were all having a bad day that day and I was worried sick about you all, especially Malika. The shoot was taking forever, and there were delays all over the place. I was getting frustrated and I... I lost my cool. I started freaking out, threatening to walk out so that I could return to you all. I was hysterical. Obe pinned me to the wall, so that I didn't hurt myself or anyone else while he tried to calm me down. He was trying to help. And of course, the..." I paused, considering my word choice carefully, "person who snapped that picture saw the situation and figured he could turn it into a scandal by leaving out the context of the situation." There was another pause of contemplation on the other end of the phone. "I'm so sorry, darling. I was trying so hard to not make your lives anymore difficult than they already were, and in the process I did exactly what I set out not to do."

"Well, it isn't completely your fault, mom. Unless you can predict the future and you still let this all happen, there was no way you could have predicted any of this. Not Malika. Not the paparazzi."

I smiled sadly as tears welled up in my eyes. "Darling, I appreciate your grace. I truly do. But you are more than entitled to be angry with me for all of this. You all are. It's been a terribly unfair situation to all of you and I've done nothing to help alleviate all the pain and drama. I am so sorry. For everything. All I can do is ask for your forgiveness and promise to do better in the future."

"It's okay, mom." I could tell it wasn't, though. Amira was that daughter who had taken on the role of the peacekeeper in the house. She listened to everyone else's stories and feelings, validated them all while no one ever asked how she was feeling or allowed her to be upset when she had every right to be. "We can talk about it when you come home. Do you have any idea when you are coming back?"

"I'll be back to you all by the end of the week if not a moment before."

"Okay." I could hear the disappointment in Amira's voice. I hoped that it wouldn't take that long to get this whole mess taken care of, but I didn't want to make a promise I wouldn't be able to keep. That would only serve to make things worse. Underpromise, overdeliver.

That way, I couldn't disappoint her and my girls any further. I would only pleasantly surprise them.

"I love you, Amira."

"I love you, too, mom."

Time to put my acting skills to good use. "How is everything going at your father's?"

"They'd be better if he didn't just up and leave."

"And he's still not back?" I asked, feigning ignorance.

"Nope."

"Have you talked to him since he left?"

"Nope. I keep calling to make sure he's okay, but he doesn't pick up."

Note to self: have Oberon turn Bradley back and modify his memory with some emergency magic. "Are you three okay?"

"Well..."

Uh-oh. "Darling? What is it?"

"After dad left, Malika kinda tried to run away from home."

"What?!"

"She said she needed to see Chad really badly. She tried to hotwire dad's Lambo so that she could drive to him. I guess no one told her that you can't hotwire cars that came out after the 90's."

"How did she even figure out *how* to hotwire a car?"

"YouTube."

Oh, good gods. "Tell me she didn't seriously damage the car."

"Well, I'm no insurance claims adjuster, but... yeah, dad is gonna flip his lid when he sees what she did."

I sighed. "What has she been doing since then?"

"Dad's head security guard confiscated her phone, keys, purse, and has been watching her like a hawk. If she's tried to make another break for it, no one has told me."

Thank the gods someone was looking out for my girls. "At least she seems to be safe for now."

"Yeah. I just don't know what's gotten into her."

"I know you're worried, darling. I am, too. I'll be home as soon as I can, and maybe we can set things right."

"I hope so. She's been sulking and crying and screaming in her room ever since. She's pissed with pretty much everyone. You, Dad, me, the security guard. She even snapped at Sami yesterday, telling her to 'get the fuck away from her.'"

We needed to fix this. Fast. "Is Sami okay?"

"No. She's kinda shut herself up and hasn't been her usual boisterous self. She really seems hurt."

"You can understand why. You two have usually been so protective of Sami. I don't recall the last time you all had a fight."

"I mean, yeah, sometimes she can be a little annoying and she struggles to figure out what's appropriate in certain places and times, but even then, I would never tell her to 'get the fuck away from me'. She's just a sweet kid, so even at her worst, it's hard to be mad at her."

"I know… Do you think Sami would want to talk to me?"

"She's at her swimming lessons right now. But I can see how she feels afterwards and call you if she's up for it."

"Please do. And if she's not in the mood or too tired, just let her know that I'll be home soon and we can talk about it."

"I will. Do you also want to talk to Malika?"

"Do you think she would talk to me?"

"Honestly, I don't think so."

I could read between the lines with that statement. Malika had been trash talking me since they left. "I understand… But I do think we are all overdue for a familial conversation when I get back."

"I was gonna say the same thing. I just hope Malika is up for a civil conversation by the time that happens."

"So do I."

"Come on now, Puck," I said as I pulled the rope behind me, dragging the jackass that Titania used to call her husband.

Puck started to walk up on us when Bradley Donkey kicked fae in the stomach. Puck doubled over and grabbed faer stomach in pain. "Stupid ass," Puck spat. Bradley Donkey brayed at Puck and turned his head around. He stuck his tongue out and Puck returned the favor.

"Enough, children," I snapped at Puck and Bradley Donkey. "We're taking you on to your new home, Bradley." He brayed again and charged me.

I sidestepped him and he ran headfirst into the wall. He stumbled backwards and blinked his eyes a few times. Shaking his head, he looked back at me and hee-hawed again before huffing.

I yanked on the rope around his neck and pulled him to me. "Let's go, you ass."

"Are you talking to the donkey or me?" Puck asked.

"Both of you jackasses." I rolled my eyes and turned back around. Without another word, I yanked on Bradley Donkey's rope and led him out of the hotel room.

"Your Majesty," Puck spoke up as we walked down the hallway. "How are we going to get this thing there?" Bradley Donkey brayed again at the stab.

"We're going to walk him, of course." I turned and shot a grin at Puck that would have put the Cheshire Cat to shame. "Well, *you* are going to walk him."

"And where are you going?" Puck asked with a raised eyebrow.

"Oh, I'm going with you," I replied with a laugh. "I just won't be walking. I'll be riding the donkey."

Puck's jaw dropped. "Are you serious?"

"Public humiliation." I laughed again. "Everyone who comes up to me and asks his name will know this is Bradley Fletcher, Jackass."

Puck shook faer head. "You really don't like him, do you?"

I scoffed. "That's putting it lightly." We got on the elevator and took it down to the bottom floor. Leading Bradley Donkey through the lobby certainly got some strange looks. I didn't care though, because I was Oberon.

Once we got outside, I handed Puck the rope. "Hold on to him tightly," I instructed. "He can be a real pain in the ass." Fae nodded and took the rope.

I walked around to the side of Bradley Donkey and straddled his back. I kicked my heels into his ribs to get him walking. He brayed and took off running.

Puck, caught off guard, was pulled to the ground. True to faer level of dedication, fae never let go of the rope. Puck was dragged along the sidewalk as Bradley Donkey ran full force through a crowd of people. Those who didn't jump out of the way were plowed over by Bradley Donkey, and again by Puck.

I laughed maniacally as I rode him through the streets of Greece, Puck slapping the concrete behind us. People screamed and cursed us, but I let the adrenaline flow as I cackled.

Once we got to where we needed to turn, I kicked Bradley Donkey in the ribs, coordinating with the way we needed to turn. He brayed and turned right. Running down the alleyway we had gone through, Bradley Donkey knocked over trash cans and boxes. He sent them flying back and knocking Puck in the face and head.

"Will you slow this damned thing down!" Puck shouted

I turned and looked at fae. Laughing, I said, "No chance in hell!" Turning around, I kicked Bradley Donkey's ribs again and made him turn left down the sidewalk.

As we approached our destination, I dug my heels into Bradley Donkey's ribs. The pain of my heels caused him to hee-haw in pain as he slowed down. I smiled once he came to a stop.

Puck stood up and brushed faerself off. "Remind me not to trust you anymore," fae scoffed.

I laughed. "Oh, that level of humiliation isn't half as bad as the eternity that Bradley is about to go through."

"Just what *are* you planning?" Fae asked with skepticism in faer tone.

I nodded across the street from us. Across from us was a sign that read 'Athens Petting Zoo'. Behind the sign stood fences filled with all kinds of farm animals. Sheep and goats bleated, dogs barked, and chickens clucked. Bradley Donkey would fit right in.

Plus, he would turn out to be the oldest donkey in history one day. Immortality was its own special kind of punishment. I made some of my worst enemies immortal so they could watch their friends and family die around them.

I took the rope from Puck as fae walked up beside me. Puck shook faer head with a smile spread across faer face. "Oh, Oberon. The old immortality punishment?"

"What could be worse than being a donkey in a petting zoo for the rest of your life?" I pointed out.

We walked across the street and into the petting zoo. As we came to the ticket desk, I asked, "How do I go about donating a donkey?"

The pimple faced teenage clerk smiled a gap-toothed smile and shook their fiery red locks out of their face. "Well, I can help with that! I'm actually the owner of the zoo."

"Ah, wonderful." I smiled and yanked Bradley Donkey's rope to bring him closer. He brayed loudly and walked forward. "This is Bradley Fletcher."

"Interesting name," they replied back to me, peeking out the window at the creature standing before them. "Why are you giving Bradley up?"

"Actually," I answered as I held up a finger. "He prefers to go by Bradley Fletcher." Bradley huffed and stomped his hooves.

"Got it," they said. "And why are you giving up Bradley Fletcher?"

I sighed as I put on my best sad look. "You see, he was my ex-wife's favorite donkey for a while. She got a new donkey a few years later that became her new favorite donkey. Now I'm stuck with this one because she took off with the new one. It's just too painful to look at him every single day."

With their bottom lip puckered out, the poor teenage dirtbag bought my story. "I'm so sorry to hear that. We'll gladly take Bradley Fletcher in. How old is he?"

"About a year," I explained. "He should be a part of the zoo for a long, long time."

24
Tati

“This is the recipe for the perfume,” I explained to my previous court members. It required cashing in on every single favor I'd ever acquired, but I managed to pull many former faeries out of retirement to help. “I need you all to work your bottoms off to multiply it and the packaging while we do the photo shoot.” My current court was doing what they did best and getting me glammed up. I handed the flash card that held the perfume recipe to Peasblossom, my former lady in waiting. She was a natural born leader and the perfect person to get everyone on track to get all the work done on time. "And don't forget to leave aside an exclusive PR package for Malika."

Oberon was on the phone, schmoozing and getting people hyped for our hasty release. I had no idea who he was talking to, but he was grinning, so it must've been going well. Of course, that smile also could have been because he had an entire hors d'oeuvre platter of cocktail weenies to himself.

Finally, my glam team was done. I was wrapped in the purest of white silk, looking like a Greek goddess with a single shoulder strap and a high leg slit. My makeup was dewy and natural looking, and the silk gown was accentuated with gold jewelry like a chain to cinch in my waist. Bracelets, necklaces, and a laurel crown weaved through my hair topped it off.

Once the finishing touches were done, the photographer led me to our hastily built set. There was a white porch swing mounted in front of a green screen. There were plants arranged around the swing, along with some strings of ivy. Even without the background that was going to be photoshopped in, I could tell we were going for the nature goddess aesthetic. *Oberon, you cheeky devil.* "Where should we start?" I asked the photographer.

Before the photographer could respond, Oberon interrupted. "Do we have a name yet, Tati?" He was covering the speaker of his phone, showing that he was still talking to someone and they were the one who originally asked the question.

"Uh..." *Fuck.* I hadn't even thought about a name. It needed to be good. Perfect.

"Potent by Hastings," Oberon suddenly said.

"Yes!" It was too perfect to curb my excitement.

Oberon pulled the phone back to his ear and confirmed, "Potent by Hastings," to whoever was on the other end of the line. He turned back to me as a grin just spread across his face. I couldn't remember the last time he looked so thrilled.

Potent.

The name alone was inspiring. Instinct took over, and I struck an elegant pose. I was channeling the statues of all the gorgeous Greek goddesses that there were in Rome. I twisted my body gently, holding the poses as though I were carved from marble, just like those statues that acted as my inspiration. The photographer didn't miss a beat and started snapping pictures.

I was so consumed with the modeling process that I didn't notice Oberon sneaking up behind me. I jumped when I felt his arms wrap around my waist. "Keep on," he encouraged me and the photographer as he continued to embrace me from behind. I snuck a look at his outfit. Obviously, he didn't look like a traditional

Greek god in leather pants, a matching leather vest, and a crimson button down. And yet... the dichotomy between us was striking enough that it just might work.

But I'd just started the long process of doing damage control from that picture Bradley took. The last thing I needed was for anyone to see something that would undo all that work. "We're trying to convince the world that this is a purely professional relationship, aren't we?" I snuck a peek at the photographer, who seemed indifferent towards our behavior as they kept snapping photos. "Tilt your chin up."

Following my orders, Oberon replied, "All for the advertisements. 'Potent by Hastings. Attract your dark side.'"

I glanced at him from out of the corner of my eye. "Damn, you're good at this."

After a dozen or so more photos and a few commercial attempts, I asked, "Should we try the swing now?"

Oberon smirked. "I mean, it wouldn't be the first time we've swung. So sure."

"Oh, yes! That was terribly fun!" I gently sat down on the swing, delicately gripping the mounting chains. "With that charming couple from Scotland." That's what I loved about the Celtic Isles. Their belief in the fae kept them enthused about having experiences with us. So wonderfully open-minded.

Oberon knelt before me while I stayed on the swing and did a couple more commercial attempts with the promotional line he came up with. But it needed something more. Something to punch it up. I pointed my toe and straightened my leg out towards him. "You know what I want."

"I'm not sucking your toes again, Tati."

Oh, my gods. I asked him to experiment once, and I was still getting teased for it. With a roll of my eyes, I clarified, "Just a kiss, darling."

"As you wish, my Queen." Without further hesitation, Oberon gently gripped my foot and leaned down to kiss the bridge of my foot.

As his lips brushed my sensitive skin, I couldn't suppress the shiver that went down my spine. It felt like lightning struck through my body, rippling through my muscles. He always had that effect on me whenever he kissed me. It didn't matter where he kissed me or what kind of kiss it was. He just knew how to kiss me.

I cleared my throat, suddenly remembering where I was and how many eyes were watching. There was no way they couldn't see the blush on my cheeks. Not with the heat that I could feel radiating off of my face. "Yes... um..." I struck a new pose on the swing, encouraging the photographer to keep going.

With a chuckle, Oberon stood and said, "Finish the shoot without me. We have enough for the darkness campaign." He started walking off the set.

No. Don't go yet. "Are... Are we sure? You can never have too many backups."

Oberon turned back to me, dropping his glasses so that he could peer at me from over the dark frames. I knew that look in his eyes. It was a look I'd seen many times... and the first time I ever saw it was the night that we consummated our burning passion for one another. "Careful, Tati. We have an image to uphold. At least, for now."

The photo shoot continued for several hours, but happened faster than any photo shoot I had ever done up to that point in my life. We were already on the third set of pose ideas. The swing was struck from the set and I took my place lying amongst the plants, lounging as though I were in nirvana itself.

Throughout the day, I kept sneaking glances over at Oberon. My team kept shooting him warning glances, which he, of course, met with his trademark immaturity. He actually stuck his tongue out at Lark, who was glaring at him from over her clipboard. There was, however, a moment where I caught Puck whispering to Oberon. It didn't take a genius to figure out that there was something else going on. I couldn't help but feel that something was inherently wrong. I tried to ignore it and just do my job, but it wasn't easy. Considering all that had happened, if something was seriously wrong, it meant that the entire world could be at risk.

"Ms. Hastings," Lark called to me. "Your phone keeps ringing from an unknown number."

I looked at the photographer. "Do you mind if we take a break?"

"Not at all," he permitted with a nod and ordered his team to take five. I stood from my lounging position and approached Lark, taking my phone from her. I answered and greeted, "This is Tati."

"So you finally figured it out?" I looked at Oberon, who had concern written all over his face. I confirmed his worries by mouthing 'Mab' to him. And then, I just hung up. "Fuck her."

"What?" Oberon asked.

"She just called to taunt me. As she does."

"Goatfucker," Oberon cursed under his breath.

My phone started vibrating again, displaying the same number that I had just answered. I tossed it back to Lark and requested, "Don't let me look at that for a day, will you, dear?"

"Lark, give me the damn phone," Oberon demanded.

My right-hand fairy looked to me for permission. I had no idea what he had planned, but after how he had taken care of me during our entire trip, I had gained a bit of trust for him. I knew he would be able to handle her. So I nodded.

Lark handed the phone to Oberon just as it started to ring again. He answered and put it on speakerphone while my glam team took advantage of the lull in action to reapply my makeup and fix my hair. "What do you want from us, Mab?"

"I want the both of you to quit what you're doing." Big surprise.

"And just why in the ever-loving fuck would we do that? We're getting ready to destroy you."

"Not if I destroy the two of you first, my dear brother-in-law."

"What the hell are you talking about?"

I answered on Mab's behalf. "She's bluffing. She talks a good game, but she never has the guts or the resources to do any real harm."

"I'm going on national television with the revelation of just who the two of you are." What an idiotic threat.

"Then you expose yourself. What are you gaining?" Nothing. Not a single soul would believe her, and even if they did, a single moment of pettiness isn't worth the cost.

"Power, my dear Oberon. If people know who I am, I'll have loyal followers. Worshippers even." Somebody's been going to the Donald Trump School of Politics.

I took over the conversation again. "First of all, you have to get the whole world to believe you. Second of all, even if you manage to convince people of the truth, don't you think we'll have just as many followers and 'worshippers'[]? You need to be paying closer attention to the Witchtok community." That alone was an army.

"There's my sweet baby sister. I don't have to get them to believe me. All I have to do is show them the footage of you and Oberon using your powers to murder people. You don't think the world will look at the two of you as the villains?"

I shrugged. "Leaked footage from a secret movie project. Oberon here wants to dabble in acting and movie making. If you don't think I can spin the yarn to tell whatever tale I want, sister, you're greatly underestimating me. I control the tabloids even better than Princess Di."

Mab let out a cackle, and as much as I tried to not let it, it unsettled me. "One step ahead of you, sweet sister. When you get back to the US, there are going to be charges filed against Obe by family members of all the people you've killed. I tracked each one of them down and showed them the footage and passed it along to the local police. There are countless warrants against you, Oberon."

That was when the room fell silent and still. Oberon... killed people? He almost never went that far when we were rulers in Greece. He only ever made that choice when there was no other option. So what was Mab talking about?

"You bitch," Oberon hissed. "How long have you been following me?"

"Oh, sweet boy." Mab chuckled again. "I don't follow you. I pay other people to follow you, yes, but you're not worth my time."

"Answer the question, Mab!" Oberon demanded.

"Long enough to know, Obe."

I'd had enough. I walked up to Oberon and snatched the phone out of his hand, disappearing into the studio bathroom and locking the door behind me. I clicked the speaker off and held the phone up to my ear. "What game are you playing?

"You don't know what he did, do you?"

"What did he do?"

"He killed my family, Tati. My mortal family. The one from when I tried to be like you."

"I didn't even know you had a family."

"Because he killed them before you could ever meet them."

"And why would he do such a thing?" Oberon was many things, but a heartless, crazed killer wasn't one of them.

"It was fifty years from the day that you left him." *Oh, gods. Exposition.* "He blamed me. He took them from me because he blamed me for losing you. He killed them while I was working in the factory. All these years, he thought he took them from me and left me wondering who killed them. But I've always known. Since then I've followed him to make sure I had everything I needed to take him down. He left me with nothing but rage and vengeance in my heart."

"And what proof do you have of your suspicions?"

"My neighbor was one of the first film majors and recorded the whole thing." She sounded so confident.

"And why should I believe you? All the lies you've told. The way you hurt my own family on purpose, I might add."

"I have the footage, dear sister."

"An easy trick of the eye, created by you. Isn't that your forte? Trickery?"

Mab chuckled again. "Come see it for yourself, sister. You know where to find me." And with that, she was gone.

I knew. I knew what Mab was going to tell Titania. Well, I knew the truth that she would base her twisted lie on. It was one of my darkest secrets and a horrific time that I lost more control than normal.

With a crack of the door, Titania stepped out of the bathroom. Eyes closed, she said to her court members and those amongst us, "Leave us."

I couldn't help but to hang my head. As the sound of feet shuffling past echoed through my brain, I glanced at the judgmental faces of her court members. I imagined some of them knew the treacherous act I had committed all those years ago. Some pitied me, but most scowled with admonished looks.

"Murderer."

"Murderer!"

Once the door closed behind the last member of her staff, I looked at Titania and said, "Yes." Her eyes searched mine as she contemplated her next move, while simultaneously probably trying to guess my game. "It's true," I confirmed. "I'm sure whatever she said was true."

Titania raised an eyebrow and nodded her head. "You murdered her mortal family because you blamed her for our separation?"

Of course she twisted it. "Okay, when you put it that way, I can understand why you're upset." I took a deep breath and clasped my hands together. "But did she tell you exactly what happened? How she set me up?" I watched Titania as her gaze never faltered. She stared into my soul, searching. Searching for the truth in my words. "How she would randomly appear in my life on the day we separated every single year to taunt me? How about how she invited me to her house that day?"

"And that warranted murdering her mortal family?" She asked, squinting her eyes and turning her head slightly to the side. "Because she was trying to be happy in the wake of our separation?"

"She lured me there by telling me that you wanted to talk to me. She told me you wanted to fix things!" I tried to explain, my voice pleading, my knees beginning to buckle.

Her face reddened as she burst out, "So you killed her family?! Because she lied like she *always* does?"

I dropped my head as the tears welled up and I fell to my knees. My hands caught my fall and I looked up at her from all fours. "Her husband shot me as soon as I got there." She was silent. My heart raced like a horse in the Kentucky Derby. "With a 12-gauge shotgun. Point blank. As soon as I opened the door, he was standing there. I nearly died that day. I had a hole in my stomach! Of course, I killed the man. I went into a blind rage and killed her entire family because I was in a dark place. I embraced my darkness for the first half a century after our separation. I did fucked up things, Titania. I'm not perfect..."

Titania walked up to me and sank to her knees. Her hands worked their way down the front of my shirt, unbuttoning each gold button.

I looked down at Titania and cocked an eyebrow. Realizing what she was doing, I bit my lip and took her hand. I traced her finger along a circular scar outlining my abdomen. If it hadn't been for Puck, I would have died that day.

I felt her body stiffen as she touched the scar. She chanced a glance up at me. "I'm sorry I never told you," I apologized with a sigh. "But it was the one thing I did that I was ashamed of after we separated."

"Why?" Titania asked, staring deep into my eyes trying to find an answer. To find hope in that dark soul of mine. "Why would she have her husband hurt you like this?"

"Because, I hurt you." I half-laughed and said, "I never said I blamed her for what she did. I hurt you in more ways than one, and I deserved to die that day."

Titania stood and backed up, resting her weary body against the wall. She closed her eyes and collapsed to the floor, pulling her knees to her chest. She looked over at me and murmured, "You know why it's so difficult being the sane faerie Queen ruling over a bunch of tricksters?"

"Why?"

Titania sighed and looked away. "Because it's impossible to find the truth. Everyone is lying or at least omitting important facts. And everyone, to some extent, is at fault. There is no black and white. Just an endless sea of gray."

I crawled toward her. Once I was in front of her, I gently turned her head so I could look into her eyes and tilted my head to the side. "Isn't that life, Titania?"

She chuckled sadly. "Yes. You want to do the right thing. But it's hard to figure out what that is. Mab should not have hurt you like that. She should have stayed out of my love life like I had told her to do so many times. But her family didn't deserve to die." I winced at her words. "But just because her family *did* die doesn't excuse her actions now. I either do nothing and the world is doomed. Or I side with my repeat offending sister who I know is a liar and a manipulator, but whom I love all the same and the world is doomed. Or I side with you..."

I rested my forehead against hers and offered, "And at least then there's hope that the world isn't doomed."

She froze at my touch and paused for a moment before she spoke. "Well I suppose that settles that. It's not like starting over is completely foreign to us."

"We have a lot to relearn about one another and forgive one another for," I confessed. "But that's all for the future. For the present, we need to get this line launched."

Titania lifted both of our heads up and looked at me. "She'll ruin us. Everything we've worked for. She has footage of you..." she drifted off. "Which I'm sure has been edited to make it look like you weren't acting in self-defense."

"Then I'll go back into hiding for another hundred thousand years!" I shouted. I would risk anything to save the world and give Titania her family back. "But I won't let her hurt you or your family with this madness any longer."

Titania took my face between her hands and stared into my eyes. Her lips crashed into mine and my eyes went wide. Once I realized what was happening, I closed my eyes and returned her kiss.

As soon as I began to reciprocate, she pulled back and gasped. I slowly opened my eyes and bit my lip. I wrapped my hand in her short pink pixie cut and pulled her back to my lips. She wrapped her arm around my head and I fell into her.

Titania hastily started removing my unbuttoned jacket and shirt. Once my top half was naked, I wrapped her in my arms and rolled us onto our sides. I ripped the goddess toga off her body and she dug her red nails into my back. The sting of her nails digging into my back caused my cock to harden in ecstasy. Crimson blood matching her fingernails creeped out from the broken skin.

"When do we need this photoshoot done?" She mumbled against my lips.

My lips moved gently against hers as my hands ran up and down her body. I sat up and looked at her. "It can wait." As I stood, I scooped her up and took her to one of the couches on set. I laid her naked body down and admired the beauty of her curves. Seeing her bare body in all its glory for the first time in over a hundred years was enough to nearly bring me to a peak. Every rolling valley reminded me of home. She was home.

I unzipped my pants and looked down at her with a burning passion. Every fiber of my being was aching to be finally back inside of her. She spread her legs apart, revealing herself to me in confirmation of what we both wanted and a silent invitation.

A look of horror crossed her face, and she said, "We need to send the crew away."

I huffed. "Aren't they far enough away?"

"They'll check on us," she tried to reason with me. "We need to make it clear work is done for the day."

"Let them check on us," I replied with a boom in my voice. I looked down at her with pure ecstasy and animalistic hunger. "I've been waiting over a hundred years for this."

I positioned myself in between her spread legs, one foot on the floor and the other propped between her and the couch. "Are you sure this is what you want, Titania?"

Her breath hitched as she paused. I could see the thoughts of family swirling through her mind. "Yes," she finally admitted.

No longer able to contain my century-long desire for her body, I wrapped my fingers around her throat and brought my stubble to her ear. "Do you remember your safe word?" I longed for my Queen's submission once more. I wanted to be her King again.

Already, her eyes started to glaze in wanton desire. "Kelpie," she whispered shyly.

I nodded and slowly slid my cock inside of her, letting her body adjust with every slight thrust. She let out a gasp that shook the room with the overwhelmed unleashing of her power. Her legs naturally made their way around me and urged my body forward. My eyes rolled into the back of my head as I relished the feeling of my beloved after all these years. It was all I had wanted for so long. Her warmth and softness combined with the beauty of our love put on a passionate display of desire. I softly groaned her name as I thrust inside of her.

"Fuck," she whimpered with a moan. She grabbed fistfuls of the couch, her blood-stained nails tearing into the fabric.

I crashed my lips down on hers and thrust slowly as our tongues met and tangled in the dance of the faeries. I let go of her waist and traced her stomach with one finger, brushing her skin with feather-light touches. Each soft stroke brought goosebumps to her skin.

She reached up and grabbed a fistful of my hair. I jerked my head back, breaking the kiss, and chewed on my bottom lip as I let out a hungry growl of her name. The feeling of her hand running through my hair was euphoric, a feeling I hadn't realized I missed so desperately. "I can't remember the last time I was on the bottom," she purred as she breathed heavily.

I chuckled as I pulled my head back and looked down at her, pausing my thrust to remain still inside of her and enjoy how it felt to have her around me. "I can't either, and I don't know when we'll do this again," I confessed breathlessly. "But I don't want to miss this opportunity."

She let out a growl. "You ass."

I snickered and pushed deeper inside of her with a forceful thrust. She yelped as I filled her even more, my cock completely sheathed within her. My hand went to one of her breasts and I massaged her nipple between two of my fingers until it had hardened and perked up at my touch. She arched her body into mine as her eyes went wide with the added stimulation of my touch. "That's just not fair."

My hand left her nipple and ran down the curves of her body. The goosebumps from my previous touch revived as I ran my hand down her porcelain skin. The other hand worked its way down between us, one finger slowly pushing along the top of my cock and into her core to stretch her open even further.

She let out a scream and arched her back. "Life isn't fair, Titania," I teased, the back of my finger rubbing against my shaft. My hand rocked as I began thrusting once more. Each thrust was followed by my thumb slowly massaging her clit, my finger dancing inside of her as my cock worked on filling her.

"Fuck!" She screamed out as I continued to thrust into her with both my hand and length. The movement of my hips was slow and subtle, but the depth of my member made her shudder as I pushed against her cervix.

She slapped a hand over her mouth to stifle another scream as her cheeks reddened darkly.

I inhaled her scent as I leaned my head down to her chest, running my tongue along the valley of her breasts. Beads of sweat dripped off my brow onto her, mingling with her own. "I've missed feeling you," I panted, my breath tickling her glistening skin as I tilted my head up to look at her.

"I've missed you too," she whispered breathily as her gaze met mine.

I thrusted passionately and worked a second finger inside her. I fully embraced her magnificent form, leaning my body into hers. My tongue traced along her pulse point, tasting her vanilla skin in my mouth after all these years. I grazed my teeth against her neck and kissed my way to her ear. I nibbled on her ear, drawing sounds of pleasure from her. "If you keep doing that..." she whimpered.

I licked along the shell of her ear. Teasing the coarse hair adorning my chin against her smooth skin, I pulled back and looked up at her with a devilish smile. "You're gonna do what?"

"I'm gonna come!" She exclaimed.

I grunted, letting my hips push into her. A low growl rumbled from my throat. "You have my permission."

Titania let out a scream, shaking the room with another eruption of her power as she finished. The warmth of her juices coated the cushion beneath us.

Her eyes rolled back as her thighs trembled against my waist. The way her walls pulsed around my shaft was something I relished as I let go of my control and came inside of her.

I collapsed on top of her and her body went limp as she stared up at me with hooded eyes. "I love you, Titania." My breath hitched as I looked down at her. She didn't verbally respond, but I could see the sentiment written across her face as she wrapped her arms around me. I snuggled into her warmth and inhaled her scent.

"You always get your way, don't you?" She huffed quietly, looking down at my head snuggled between her bare breasts.

"One way or another, we always find our way back to one another," I murmured against her skin.

There was no time to rest after the photo shoot. Oberon and I had to get to the airport almost immediately, leaving both of our teams behind to finish duplicating the product and to ship out the PR packages. We were just barely going to make it to New York in time for the announcement and interviews.

The hustle of getting on the jet made it easy to avoid Oberon. Even once we were settled on the aircraft, he was so consumed by his work editing our photos that he didn't even try to entertain a conversation.

Good. I had no idea what to say. And that was rare for me.

In less than twenty-fours, I had become a liar to my daughters. Oh, I had lied before, of course. I lied about who I was to the world and to them. I lied about my age, even more so than was typical for women in my profession. I lied to them about what was wrong with Malika. I lied about how I came to know Oberon. Those lies were necessary for me to live my life and for them to live theirs.

But I always swore I would never lie to them about the important things. I didn't lie to them. They heard Bradley and I fighting. I told them that mommies and daddies fight sometimes, and we were each going to talk to people about our fights to try and fix them. I didn't lie to them when I stopped loving Bradley for good. Instead, I told them that therapists and counselors couldn't help us and that their father and I were going to be better people and parents to them once we went our separate ways. I didn't lie to them when I started dating Chad before our divorce was finalized. I told them that mommy was trying to meet new people, make new friends, and was starting to really like one or two of them. And after an initial meeting with each new stranger to make sure that they were safe for all of us and that we were both on the same page of interest, the second meeting was always reserved for introducing my girls to my new friends and lovers. Chad was the first one that made it past my girls and the background check.

No, I wasn't a perfect mother, and there were times where lying to them was absolutely necessary. But I never lied when I didn't have to.

Except for now. And I didn't even know I had lied until it was too late.

I had promised Amira that I wasn't cheating on Chad with Oberon. I had promised her. And at the time, it was the truth. I never thought I would ever feel this way about Oberon again. The damage had been done centuries ago, and I truly didn't think that either of us could ever get past those damages. Oh, friendship was always possible; the world was lonely for the immortal fae. We were few and far between, and obviously I wasn't going to find any companionship with my sister. So Oberon and I were bound to gravitate towards one another, eventually.

I just didn't think it would happen so soon. Or that it would be anything more than friendship ever again.

I still didn't know what the hell came over me. One minute I was coming to the frightening realization that my sister had convinced her husband, the brother-in-law I never got to meet, to try to kill my multiple-times ex-husband. That same ex-husband of mine ended up killing the man and Mab's children, my niblings who I also never knew existed, in enraged self-defense.

And all of that had happened decades ago, and I never knew. None of them told me. Did it make sense that no one ever said a word? I suppose, knowing everyone who was involved. But it was still infuriating to know that I was kept in the dark about those serious events. I deserved to know.

And because I didn't know, I was now having to process all of that information while on a fifteen hour flight back to the States. I had to go through the grieving process for the extended family I never met. I had to process the anger I had for Mab and her husband for trying to harm Oberon. I had to process the empathy I felt for my sister after losing her family. And I had to process the almost irrational fear I had at the idea of losing Oberon. And never knowing it almost happened.

When Oberon and I had finally parted ways so long ago, I said a lot of things in anger. The least of which was that I never wanted to see him again. I never thought some force in the universe would take me up on that request. Least of all, my sister.

And after all this time, I was finally starting to understand how little I genuinely meant of those hard words. I didn't live with many regrets in life. And now, I was being bombarded with regret, among all the other strong feelings that were hitting me all at once.

Fifteen hours would not be enough to work through all of those emotions and still be presentable for the launch in New York City.

What had happened? In less than a week, the perfect life that I was leading had turned completely upside down. Nothing made sense anymore.

And I was supposed to go back to that perfect life with nothing making sense anymore.

It hadn't occurred to me until that precise moment that Oberon and I wouldn't have much time left together. The flight, the launch, and then the flight back to L.A. Maybe twenty-four hours at most. And then we would have to go our separate ways. I would go back to Chad, my girls, and my acting career. He would go back to his company.

If our lives weren't completely ruined by Mab first.

Yes, I needed to start making contingency plans for that. Whatever incriminating evidence there was would mostly affect Oberon, but I wasn't going to come out of it unscathed. Mab wouldn't let me. I was going to lose something in this... Something more than just Oberon.

Maybe she or someone who worked for her would call CPS and have my children taken away from me because I was fraternizing with a murderer. It would probably be Bradley. I still didn't know where he was and Mab would look for allies wherever she could find them. So I needed to get my lawyer ready for a possible custody battle. Either against Bradley or against the state of California.

My career would take a hit, too, even if I managed to hang onto my children. This would only result in being canceled. Sure, there would be some who still supported me on the internet, but they would be few and they wouldn't have the power to change hearts and minds.

So I would need to find some other way to get the glamor I needed to survive. Broadway and the music industry were out of the question. Some greedy miser might have the balls to hire me if they thought my presence on stage or behind the microphone would be controversial enough to get them attention. But that was a long shot. The day of hate watchers and listeners was coming to an end, and the art of boycotting was being perfected with every generation.

I suppose YouTube and other forms of small content creator platforms were always an option. Someone would watch. Probably not enough people, but there would be an audience.

Or I could take the vast wealth I'd saved over the centuries and start my own production company. I could produce what I wanted all the time, every day. All day. 24 hours of work a day, seven days a week. But I never really was good with the "business" side of the industry. It wasn't where my joy was.

And then, of course, there was home. The forests back in Greece where Oberon and I once ruled as King and Queen. My court would follow me back there to remain at my beck and call. Our return would probably call many other members of the fae back, so we could have a true court again rather than the downgraded, minimal entourage that braved L.A. with me. We still had a few friends in other courts who would be happy to welcome us back. There would also be a few courtiers who wouldn't be so happy to see us, but they'd never had the balls to attack us even when we were away. Why would they suddenly get brave when we returned?

And Oberon would be there if I asked him to be. The man was resourceful and could start over even better than I could, so his options weren't as limited. But if I asked him to come back with me, he would. And I would have his love and devotion forever. As I always had, whether I wanted it or not.

I looked over my shoulder towards the front of the plane. Oberon sat there, hunched over his laptop, the screen reflected on his dark spectacles. He was so engrossed, so focused on what he was doing. Oh, he did have his moments of short attention spans, particularly whenever anything or anyone bored him. We'd stop going to balls and parties long ago because he was too blunt whenever someone he didn't like was telling a story that was less than engaging. But when it really

mattered, when it was something important, wild horses couldn't break his concentration.

That was one of the things I loved about him. He knew
when it all mattered.

And he knew that this definitely mattered.

A wave of exhaustion hit me on the heels of that
comforting thought. We'd been going, going, going ever
since that day in the restaurant. And while I at least had
taken the time to eat and sleep, the stresses were still
high through all of those days. My body wasn't able to
maintain that high level of anxiety anymore. Especially
not while knowing that Oberon would find a way to take
care of both of us, no matter what happened. I reclined
the luxury plane seat, got as comfortable as I could, and
closed my eyes, relishing in the fifteen hours of rest that
I could now get.

As sleep overtook me, visions of the happy times
with Oberon danced in my head. The mischief we both
caused. The children we raised. Our wedding day. After
all these years, those were still some of the happiest
moments in my life.

I still loved Oberon. No matter how much I and my
conscious mind tried to deny it.

Maybe losing everything wouldn't be so bad. So long
as we went through it together.

27

Oberon

Titania sat beside me in the green room of the talk show we were preparing for. Her glam team was painting her delicate pale skin with blushes of red and pink to match her pixie cut. As the team began on her nails, she looked over at me. "Once we do this, there's no going back," she said firmly. "And we both live with the consequences."

"The only consequence is taking down Mab." I chuckled and ran my hand through my freshly brushed hair, ruffling it for a more natural look than the stylist was going for. "And I'm always okay with that."

Titania took my hand in hers and closed her eyes. "Breathe with me," she instructed. I meditated and took deep breaths. Memories of the night before ran through my head as I felt her smooth skin against my hand. She squeezed my hand tightly as hers trembled. Gently, I rubbed the smooth side with my thumb.

We exhaled slowly and opened our eyes. I met Titania's gaze and I could tell by the look in her eyes that the same visions that flashed through my mind had gone through hers. "Whatever happens," she stated, "we face this together."

I smiled at her. "That's the way it's always been." She bit her lip, and I took it as a sign of hurt from my words. She felt like she had abandoned me, I'm sure. However, I knew better than to believe that she had. "We've got this, Titania."

We were interrupted by the stage manager bursting into the dressing room. We both looked over at the lad clad in a black suit with a bluetooth headset on his head and a clipboard and pen in hand. "Ms. Hastings, Mr. Obe," he said hurriedly. "You're on in five."

We squeezed one another's hand. "Thank you," Titania replied as she looked back at me. "Shall we?"

I nodded slowly and took a deep breath. "Let's do the damn thing, my love." Titania giggled, and we both got up to take our place backstage.

I looked around cautiously before taking a step towards Titania. I was looking for Puck, who was supposed to be there by now. Something didn't feel right. As I got next to her, Titania glanced over at me and I smiled back. "Time to shine."

She flashed me her best social media smile. "That's what I do." I took her hand and we stepped through the curtains, my free hand raised in the air as the crowd of *The Helen Show* erupted in applause. Titania was right by my side, waving, smiling, and blowing kisses. I ran my hand through my disheveled hair and pushed my cut to the opposite side of my shaved head before looking over at Helen. She smiled at me and I let go of Tati's hand to take Helen's and raised it to my lips. Gently placing a kiss on her hand, I let it go and turned back to the crowd before raising both hands to my lips and blowing the crowd a kiss.

Tati smiled wider as she kissed Helen on both cheeks while I sat down in my white seat. She whispered to Helen, "We owe you," before she took her seat next to mine. I crossed my leg across my knee and unbuttoned my suit jacket as I leaned back. Scanning the room for Puck, I glanced at the crowd through the dark lenses of my glasses.

As the LED sign above us flashed from green to red, the crowd quieted down and Helen began. "Well, this is certainly an odd pair!" The crowd let out a chuckle, and I followed suit. "How did this odd partnership happen?"

"Well, of course," Titania explained, turning to look at me. "He was the mastermind."

I smiled back at her and turned to Helen. "When the idea for Potent came to me, Tati was the first one that came to mind. I mean, look at her. Isn't she stunning?" The crowd cheered at my words, and Helen grinned.

Titania blushed and waved at the crowd playfully. "Oh hush, Obe, you're embarrassing me." The crowd let out another chuckle. "I, of course, have been using Obe's investment advice from his books and business practices for a few years now. So when I got the notice that he wanted to speak to me, I was both honored and a little intimidated."

I widened my eyes a little, pretending to be stunned. "Tati is one of the hottest stars in Hollywood," I commented. The crowd oohed. "And I mean hottest in every sense of the word. I knew she was the best one to help take the business to the next level. Her fashion and business sense helped me figure out exactly what our market wanted. She's a damn genius. Can I say damn?" The crowd let out a little laugh.

"So long as you don't say 'God' before it," Helen replied with a laugh. "We won't bleep it."

I nodded in understanding. "Duly noted. But Tati, she's wonderful. She has a nose for the perfume industry and an eye for marketing. I've been truly fortunate that she agreed to help me. If anything, I should have been the one that was honored and intimidated."

"How long did it take you to find the right scent for Potent?" Helen asked.

I looked at Titania and tilted my head to the side. "A lot of blood, sweat, and tears went into finding the right scent."

"I can't tell you how many experiments we did," Titania added. "We both lost sleep because of it."

I raised my eyebrows and chuckled. "That's putting it lightly."

"Is that why you both looked so upset in that picture that hit the internet?" Helen asked as the picture that Bradley had sold to the media flashed on the screen behind us. I turned to look at it and shifted uncomfortably in my chair as memories of that night flooded my mind.

Titania must have noticed my silence and discomfort, and chimed in. "Well, on top of all the late nights, stress, and anxiety about the project, I was, of course, missing my family terribly."

"We both were extremely stressed that night," I said, as I turned back around to face Helen. "We thought we were making progress, but it turned out we were regressing. Well, I was regressing. Tati never faltered on this journey. She's impressive."

"Oh, please." Titania laughed. "I was a complete emotional wreck, as you can see from the ugly crying in that photo."

"So tell us more about the photo," Helen pried. I knew she was a TV host and had to boost ratings, but damn she could have given us a heads up that this was going to be part of the segment. "Because the rumor when it first circulated was that you two were an item now. Is there any truth to that?"

"Oh, Helen." Titania laughed again and waved off the insinuation. She was handling this much better than I was. Or was she? "You know better than to believe everything you read."

"I could only be so lucky," I added. "That picture was a setup by a jealous ex and competition for our line. Somehow, it was leaked to the founder of Apothefairy that we were getting ready to launch and she was ..." Smoke appeared around the stage and a flash went off as the lights flickered, cutting me off.

"Hello darlings." I knew that voice before the smoke dissipated and revealed Mab in all her pitiful existence.

Titania rolled her eyes. How was she so calm on the outside? "Well, speak of the devil and she shall appear."

Mab returned the eye roll and scoffed. "Very funny, sister. But I told you not to test me."

Helen stood up and looked at her stage hands, who all shrugged. She turned back to Mab. "Excuse me, who are you?"

"I think the better question is who are these two?" Mab shot back as she pointed at Titania and me. "Maybe that's what we should be asking, Helen."

"Poor dear, can't handle competition well." Titania sighed and shot a poignant look at Mab. "So she tries to kill it before it can start."

"Speaking of killing." Mab smiled and looked me dead in the eyes. "Obe, shall we show the people who you truly are?" Where the fuck was Puck?

I stood and pointed at Mab. "Enough with this madness, Mab!" Another puff of smoke rose from the ground between Mab and me. Puck leapt from the smoke and tackled Mab to the ground.

Titania whistled and waved over her team of bodyguards and glam team to help Puck. Once the glam team got there and Puck stood up, fae walked to me and whispered into my ear. "Took longer to convince the police that she doctored it than I thought. But they finally have all the evidence they need and are on their way to arrest her now."

I smiled and nodded at Puck. When I turned to Titania, I whispered to her. "Puck collected enough evidence and turned it over to the police. They showed them how she doctored the film she was using and how she had been stalking us and threatening us. She's done."

A flurry of emotion, anger and sadness mixed with confusion and indifference flitted across her face. It was the first time I saw emotion on her face since we started the interview.

Puck walked to the center of the stage and looked over at the crowd, pulling out a bottle of Potent to reveal its look to the crowd for the first time. "Potent," fae said. "Tackle your dark side."

Helen flew out of her chair for a standing ovation. "What a reveal!"

Titania chucked to herself a little, dropping her voice to speak to me. "You certainly know how to make lemonade, don't you?"

"Life has handed me nothing but lemons," I told her. "I got damn good at making lemonade. But, this? This was all Puck's idea."

"Finally using faer powers for good, I see." Titania paused and looked over at me. "What will happen to her?"

"Worst-case scenario, she'll spend a few years in jail for insider trading and blackmailing, as well as filing a false police report. She'll lose everything she's got and have to start over again. Best-case scenario, she gets a slap on the wrist and gets out on parole while having to pay a fine. She would also have to deal with the PR storm."

Titania sighed and looked down at her feet. "I wish I knew what to hope for."

I chewed my lip, contemplating my next words. "She'll always be your sister, and I get that, but eventually she has to learn a lesson and take responsibility for her actions."

"Yes," she agreed half heartedly. "I suppose so."

"I know it isn't easy," I admitted. "But I'm proud of you for sticking with this."

"Thank you, darling." She looked back up at me and smiled a half smile. "I'm just glad that you're...." she paused and her eyes went wide. "*We're* okay."

Helen turned back to Titania and me with a wide smile on her face. "How exciting. You have an excellent PR team working with the two of you. One of the best reveals on television, if you ask me."

"Well, darling," Titania said as she slipped back into her TV personality. "You know me. I have a penchant for the dramatic. And of course, everyone in your lovely audience is going home with a bottle of Potent!"

I stood up and threw my arms out wide. "Check under your seats, all of you!"

"You get a bottle! You get a bottle! Everybody gets a bottle!" Titania cheered. I glanced over at her and she winked at me. We smiled and our gaze locked. For a minute, I swear she was telling me she loved me with her eyes.

28
Tati

'The girls are all home safe?', I texted Bear when their ETA had come.

'Yes, my lady'

'Did you get the PR package to Malika?'

'Yes, my lady.'

'And?' I asked, riddled with anxiety.

'It seems to have worked. She disappeared into her filming room to do the review, but she had barely been in there for five minutes before she came out. She was much quieter than usual and she just disappeared into her room.'

Well, that was still very out of character for her 'Leave her be. I'll talk to her when I get home.'

'Yes, my lady.'

I checked the time before putting my phone away. My limo was on its way to pick me up from the airport. With the LA traffic, I would just make it back in time for dinner. It felt like an eternity before I could see my girls. I was both excited and nervous to see them.

I looked up from my phone to see Oberon was at the front of the plane, watching the news. Mab's on air arrest was the top story across all social media. It was a great benefit to us that her shenanigans interrupted our launch announcement. We were trending right along with her, and every story about her automatically had our names and product attached to it.

For all intents and purposes, both Oberon and I should have been popping champagne and celebrating. My daughters were all safe and back to their old selves. Our product was a best-seller, We'd foiled Mab's plan to throw the world into complete chaos. And she had completely failed at exposing us to the world. We got everything we wanted and lost nothing.

And despite all of that, we were both terribly quiet throughout the whole flight home. No champagne. No laughter. No celebration. And I could tell that Oberon was in a very deep state of depression. He was only ever quiet and still when he was depressed, and he hadn't said a word the entire flight.

Even after we landed at the airport, Oberon remained sitting, watching the news story that displayed Mab's public shame. I walked up to stand next to his still seated form. I patted his shoulder, not knowing what else to do. "Well, you're a hit, darling."

"Yeah." Not a trace of joy was in his voice. I looked down at my feet, searching for anything to say.

"So. What is next for you?" I chanced a look over at him. From behind those dark glasses, I saw no trace of life in his eyes. He was in a trance. Unfeeling. Uncaring. Not because he was incapable. But because if he wasn't, he would feel too much.

He shook his head, breaking away from whatever daydream he was engrossed in. "I'm sorry. What?"

I stepped in front of his seat, forcing him to focus on me. "Alright. What's wrong?"

Oberon cast his gaze down to the floor, doing his best to escape me and my looks. "I just," he paused, struggling to put his thoughts into words. "Mab was right, Titania." Words I never thought I'd ever hear him say in his entire immortality. I pressed the back of my hand against his forehead, feeling for any extreme temperature difference that would indicate an illness or infection. Oberon chuckled mirthlessly, brushing my hand away. "Everywhere I go, death follows. I was supposed to be a protector for the world, not Maman Brigitte."

A loa of death. Hadn't heard that name in far too long. I wondered if she was still running that distillery. I hoped so. That hot pepper rum she made was too good to be lost to time. "Okay, first of all, you know how nice Brigitte is."

"She is, she is," Oberon agreed, waving me off. "You get my point."

I did. It wasn't a comment on Brigitte's character.

But that didn't stop me. "Second, darling, we're immortal. We have the terrible task of protecting the world. And sadly, we fuck it up. And we're going to every century or so. Death doesn't follow you, Oberon. How could you possibly have predicted that Mab would be so unhinged as to try to kill you?"

"I should have known better. I should have known it was a trap."

I smoothed the back of my dress so that I could squat down before him and force his downcast eyes to look at me again. "Darling, I couldn't have predicted such an act from her, and I'm her damn sister. If I couldn't predict it, how could you?"

Oberon sighed. "Because I should have known that, after fifty years, you wouldn't want to talk to me. Hell,

Titania, the only reason I got your attention this time was because the world was on the verge of pure chaos."

Well, that, I didn't have an argument for. What could I say to that? It was that truth. If Mab hadn't been up to no good at the time, I don't think I would have entertained any of the time I spent with Oberon. It was my turn to look at the ground, unable to find anything appropriate to say.

"But," Oberon continued as he stood up and stepped away from me towards the front door of the plane. "Rightfully so. I was a pompous ass, the very thing that I turned everyone into. I was projecting my own self-worth on those I deemed less worthy of your attention, but really it was me who wasn't deserving of your attention."

Everything he said was true. That was why I left. Every accusation Oberon made during our marriage was a confession. And I eventually couldn't take it anymore. But in the short time we'd spent together, I hadn't seen a single trace of that man. Not even during our confrontation with Bradley.

I stood up from my squatting position. "It's not like we haven't stepped away only to come back together a hundred times over." I had to test the waters before we were out of time. I wouldn't be able to live with myself if I didn't.

"You have a family you have to get back to, Titania." Yes. Yes, I did. And a fiancée who was probably thoroughly confused by everything that had happened in the past week and who I didn't know if I could return to authentically. But that was Oberon's answer. And it spoke volumes with so few words.

I straightened my dress. "Yes. And you have a company that I'm sure is a wreck without you."

"Sadly, you're right. The mortals can't handle simple investments. It's like they're incompetent when it comes to the concept of bartering and transactional deals."

I had always wondered why Oberon would go into something so boring as finance and cryptocurrency, but that statement made sense. We fae loved cutting a good deal. Especially when it came with loopholes and pitfalls we could take advantage of. "Right."

Oberon led me off the plane, offering a hand going down the stairs. "What're your plans from here?"

"Well, I have to make sure my daughters are okay. Especially Malika. I'm gonna have to figure out what to tell them about Bradley."

"Oh, I've already turned him back and made him forget everything after he met Mab. As far as he knows, he was in a boating accident that caused memory loss." That was surprising. I was positive that Oberon had done something to make sure the man was permanently missing.

"Yes-"

Before I could say anything else, Puck appeared from the back of the plane. And I know for a fact fae didn't board with us back in New York. "Oberon, there's a fire at the office."

"What's going on now? What could possibly not wait until I got back?"

"There's a fire." Even I could have figured that one out.

"I heard you the first time. What kind of fire, Puck?"

"The hot kind." That is how I knew Oberon wasn't in a good mental state. He wasn't able to recognize Puck's dry humor.

It was at that precise moment that Bear rolled up in my limo. As Oberon sighed and turned back to me, I said what he didn't have the strength to say. "You'd better go."

"Yes, I suppose so."

But don't go. "I suppose I'll see you around town."

Before I could make a move to hug or kiss my ex-husband, Oberon stuck his hand out for a handshake. "It's been a pleasure working with you, Tati Hastings."

I tried to ignore the stinging pain that blossomed in my heart at the standoffish, professional gesture. I took his hand and shook it weakly. "You too, Obe."

For a moment, I thought Oberon was going to say something else. Something that I hoped was on both of our minds. I could tell he wanted to say something with the way he kept looking in my eyes for far too long. But rather than give into that urge, he released my hand and turned back to Puck. "Puck, pull the car around."

Puck nodded and leapt over the metal banister of the plane stairs and disappeared again before fae could land.

Oberon and I lingered a bit longer at the foot of the staircase before Oberon broke away to collect his luggage and settle up with the pilot.

I, on the other hand, kept standing there on the tarmac until Bear exited the limo and approached me. "Ms. Hastings?"

"Yes, I suppose we should go." I reluctantly followed Bear back to my limo, sliding into the back seat with another backward glance to Oberon. His back was to me, and that was a deliberate move on his part. He didn't want to put himself through the same pain I was feeling at that moment.

Once the limo door was closed behind me, I rolled up the partition between Bear's driver's seat and my passenger area. I didn't want him to see or hear me as I released the whirlwind of emotions out of my body. Thank goodness the windows of the limo were tinted so that everyone else couldn't see my breakdown.

I perched myself on the back seat, looking out the back window at Oberon. As we rolled away from the airport, I refused to take my eyes off of my King of the Faeries until he was no longer in sight.

29

Oberon

"You fool."

"You let her walk away?"

"You failed given the opportunity to win her back."

I took a deep breath as I stood there, looking at the gate of the California Correctional Institution. I was there to see Mab. The prison's warden owed me a favor, and I was taking him up on that in order to speak my final peace.

I walked to the guardhouse and knocked. The warden greeted me at the door with a bow. "Your Majesty." He smiled at me. "What has it been, a couple thousand years?"

"Since I saved your faerie ass from the Minotaur?" I laughed. "I warned you against testing the Fates, but you wouldn't listen to me."

"Have I ever listened to the Royal Court?" He chuckled.

"I suppose not." I sighed as my face sobered, all smiles and joking replaced with a frown. "I need to see Mab."

The warden cocked his head to the side and chewed his lip. "That is a mighty high favor, Your Majesty."

"Higher than saving your life?" I quirked an eyebrow and slightly turned my head.

He sighed. "I suppose not." He closed the door behind him. "Come on, I'll lead you to her cell."

I nodded. "Thank you."

"I will warn you, she's been a bit mad since she arrived," he cautioned as he turned around with a serious look drawn across his face.

"Hasn't she always been mad?" I laughed.

His stoic expression never changed. "No, Your Majesty, I mean she has been especially mad. She's talking to herself, ranting about you and Titania. She's in restricted housing because she couldn't keep her hands to herself. Prison riots, staff assaults, you name it. It has been a challenge to control her, I'll be honest."

My face dropped as I realized she was an immortal faerie who had powers and could easily mutilate half the prison if she got out of control. I shuddered and shook my head slowly. "Alright then," I said before taking a deep breath. "Well, we should go see her before she breaks out." I was half-joking, half being serious. He nodded and turned around to lead me through the prison.

"She almost killed you once."

"She'll kill you this time."

"You're poking the bear, Oberon."

"What are you going to do? Murder her?"

"Of course, you're a murderer."

"Enough!" I yelled out.

The Warden jumped and turned around. He looked at me with a raised eyebrow and pursed lips. "What do you mean, Your Majesty?"

I shook my head. "Nothing, talking to myself."

He chuckled and turned around. "Sounding like Mab there for a second." If he only knew the extent of how I talked to myself. We rounded a corner and came to one last door. The Warden pulled out his radio and whispered a code that wasn't audible to me. Clanking metal moved within the door and the Warden pulled it open.

The circular room was accented by five doors. Five restricted housing rooms. I glanced at the names on the door. Kenny Seaform, Poly Femus, Mab... There she was. I walked to the door and slid open the sliding window on the door to reveal the metal grates and shield separating us.

"Mab?" I asked as I peered through the window and stared at a seemingly empty, white concrete room.

Suddenly, her face appeared in front of the window, and I was peering into her dilated eyes. "Oberon," she hissed, her tongue flicking like a snake. "I was wondering when you would show your pitiful face. How'd you do it?"

"It wasn't me." I smiled. "It was Robin."

She rolled her eyes. "Of course, that little Puck fuck was the cause of my demise." She scoffed. "I underestimated him."

"Fae," I corrected.

"I'm sorry?" She blinked rapidly and tilted her head back.

"Faer pronouns are fae/faer," I informed her.

"Fine." She huffed. "How did *fae* do it?"

"Easy, I taught faer about the magic-science explanation," I began. "Fae decided to use the illusion charm on the video. Every single copy of the video you had stored in your office." Her eyes went wide. "While you were busy stalking us and following us, Puck had ample opportunity to sneak into your office and cast an illusion spell. Then, for safe measure, fae put an illusion spell on the eyes of all the California police, FBI, SBI, and most of the law enforcement across the United States to see the same thing. Fae couldn't alter the video, but fae could make sure everyone saw what fae wanted them to see."

"What do you have left, Obe?" She hissed.

Nothingness was all that I had left. "More than you'll ever have behind this door."

"*Enough!*" She cried as her eyes bulged out of her head and she started looking around her cell. Mab punched the door, the metal bending outward.

"Stop, Mab," I demanded, trying to calm her down. She continued to punch the door as tears streamed down her cheeks. "Mab, enough!" I shouted.

She let out an ear-piercing scream that buckled my knees. I slapped my hands over my ears to block out the sound. I pulled out a scroll from my pocket and unrolled it. "By Order of Titania, Queen of the Faeries, you are hereby stripped of all titles and any benefits, material or otherwise, that those titles would bestow on you."

Her voice quieted to a normal level. She stopped and looked at me, blinking rapidly. "What?"

"Your powers are gone, Mab," I explained. "Titania has stripped you of all the benefits that come with being a faerie. Including your powers and immortality." Her eyes went wide and her jaw dropped. "You're done, Mab. Reap the benefits of your creation."

"No," she whispered, voice barely above a mouse squeak. "No, no, no, no!"

When Bear and I finally arrived home, Chad was waiting in the driveway with his yellow Jeep. It didn't take a genius to figure out what was happening. The back seat was full of various items that had slowly made their way into my home since our relationship started. His guitar case, a few conversation pieces that ended up in my foyer, and a pile of suitcases that no doubt held all of his clothes that had ended up in my closet or in my laundry.

"Ms. Hastings?" I knew what Bear was trying to ask without him verbalizing it.

"Take my bags inside. I'd like to have a moment alone with him."

"Yes, Ms. Hastings." Bear helped me out of the limo and then tended to my bags. Leaving me to stand awkwardly in the driveway, wondering how this reunion needed to go, considering the inevitable.

"Hey," I said sheepishly as I stepped up to Chad.

"Hey," Chad returned. He was trying to make me feel better with a smile, but I could tell it was to hide the sad awkwardness that seemed to consume him now. I could feel his energy on the exact same frequency as mine. Nervous and struggling to do the right thing. We tried to hug, testing the waters to see if there really was no going back to the way things were. Where once his free spirit wrapped around me like warm honey, now he was stiff and cold like ocean driftwood. And I knew he could feel the same thing in my body.

Breaking the hug, I looked back at the Jeep's back seat, filled with the remains of our love. *I'm too old to play dumb anymore*, I thought to myself, dismissing the idea that I could ask what was going on as if I didn't already know. "So," was all I could think to say.

"So," Chad repeated. "Look, Tati. I know you had no control over what happened. We were both really shocked at how Malika started behaving, and it's not your fault at all. I tried to keep that in mind and tried to tell myself that this was just a hiccup and there are gonna be plenty of those in our marriage because, well, that's life. It's full of hiccups, and I've always managed to make it through the hiccups.

"But," Chad paused, struggling to find the words that would cause the least amount of pain to me. "Well, the girls deserve a father who will be able to always be there for them, especially when they're going through a rough time. This was my opportunity to do that for them. For Malika... and I couldn't handle it."

Rather than interrupting with some words of pity and empty reassurance, I stayed quiet and listened to what he had to say. "I mean, I wanted the girls to like me one day. Maybe not to the point of seeing me as their dad, but enough to want to talk to me. And I thought that was gonna take a long time and effort, and I was ready to put that time and effort in. But..." Chad took a long moment to consider his words carefully. "I never would have imagined that them liking me *too* much would have ever been an issue we would have to face. And when I needed your help to deal with all this, you weren't there. You ran away. I know you were contractually obligated months in advance, but... it still sucked to have to deal with this alone. And I'm not sure that I believe it was just the legal obligations that made you go."

A thinly veiled accusation like that had sent me into rages in the past, even when they were absolutely true. Oberon, Theseus, Bradley. I always had a reason to blame them for my attention turning elsewhere. *"You did it, so I can too." "I have needs that you're not fulfilling anymore." "At least he treats me with respect."* Their poor behavior was always the defense for my choices. And I would defend myself with screaming vitriol.

But not this time. Chad had done nothing to earn the awkward situation he found himself in; becoming the uncomfortable item of my daughter's affection while I was off, fucking Oberon for all he knew. For all he correctly knew.

He was in the wrong place at the wrong time with Malika. That wasn't a crime. And just because I didn't go to Greece intending to hurt Chad doesn't mean that I didn't hurt him.

"I love you, Tati. I love you enough to want you to be happy, even if it's not with me. And I love myself enough to walk away and find someone who will be happy with me. And in the meantime, I'll just love myself enough to be happy on my own."

There should have been tears. Some kind of shattering in my chest as the painful truths came into understanding. I should have felt some kind of pain, even if I was in complete agreement with the choices he was making. But there was nothing. There was a sense of relief that he had the bravery to do what I couldn't.

There was a relaxation that there was, frankly, one less thing to try to juggle perfectly in my life. And there was something I couldn't put a name to yet. But it wasn't pain, hurt, sorrow, or heartbreak.

"Are you going to be okay?" I asked with genuine concern.

"Oh, I'll be fine," he replied with a shrug. "I may have to write a song or two about it to process it all. I hope that's okay."

"Of course, it is, darling. I know they'll be just as brilliant as you."

He gave a sad laugh. "Thanks. I'll try to not be too harsh."

"Be as harsh as you need to be. It's your healing, and I'm a big girl. I can accept the consequences of my actions."

Chad nodded again. "I better get going. You need to talk to the girls, I'm sure, and I..." He didn't have a reason why he had to leave, other than that he wanted to leave. And that was reason enough. "Yeah."

Taking a hint from how stiff the hug was, I knew better than to ask for another. Instead, I removed the engagement ring from my finger and handed it back to him. The first engagement ring I had ever given back. Chad gave a small smile that was genuine, not born in sadness or covering discomfort. His face just brightened as I put the diamond-studded metal into his warm hand. "No matter what anyone says, Tati, you're a real class act."

I smiled at the genuine compliment, happy that Chad didn't completely hate me even so soon after my betrayal of him. "I was gonna say that about you, dear."

We held hands for a long moment before Chad released his grip first. "Goodbye, Tati."

"Goodbye, Chad."

31
Oberon

I sat at the airport alone once again. I had relinquished control of the business to Puck. I trusted that fae would know how to continue the success of the business I had worked so hard to build. There was a part of me that was sad about leaving it behind. It had been my pride and joy for so long, something that I wanted to take care of and rejuvenate myself.

"Just like your marriage, running away until the very end."

"You're a failure, Oberon."

"A weak coward, afraid of everything that moves."

I slammed my eyes shut and slowly rubbed my temples in a clockwise motion. I wanted to force those voices away. It seemed like the farther I got away from Titania, the louder they grew. They forced their poison into the madness of my mind, silencing any semblance of sanity that still existed within me.

I wasn't sure how I was going to make it through the rest of my immortal life without Titania. But the way we left things proved there was no hope left for our reconciliation. Any chance we had of working things out was quickly squashed when I left her with a mere handshake. I knew I had royally screwed that up, but at the same time wondered if I actually had. What if she didn't reciprocate the feelings of renewed love and newfound desires that I felt for her? She could have easily dismissed me with any loving gesture I made towards her. I would never know now.

"You ruined your chances."

"You'll never win her back."

I stood up and paced back and forth along the corridor of the terminal. The smell of coffee filled my nose and pulled me to a nearby coffee shop. Walking up to the register to order my triple espresso, I noticed the TV behind the counter flashing a picture of Titania and Bradley with a red stamp across it that said *Divorced*.

My heart sank. *At least the world can know about her and Chad now.* I dropped my gaze to the barista at the counter, waiting to take my order. The thin girl at the register peered at me from behind her wireframe glasses and smiled a crooked smile. "What can I get you, Mr. Obe?"

"Triple Espresso," I replied with an exaggerated sigh. As the barista turned to make my drink, I glanced back at the TV. On the TV was a candid picture of Titania and Chad holding hands in front of a yellow Jeep. I winced at the pain in my heart as I realized the announcement of the divorce was preceded by the announcement of their engagement. Then a pair of scissors appeared on the screen and dramatically cut the picture down the middle, separating the two former lovebirds.

"Excuse me," I said to the barista.

She turned around, her purple hair flowing in the breeze of the air conditioning above her. "Yes, sir?"

"Can you turn the TV up?" I asked, my gaze never leaving the broken frame that surrounded Titania, my former lover. She nodded and reached up to the TV. With the press of a button, she brought the volume up until it was audible.

"Tati Hasting's successful new perfume launch can't protect her from all the rejection she's getting in her love life." The voice began as the tabloid-facing news channel flashed to their anchors sitting on screen. A video of Titania and Bradley standing outside Titania's house ran in the background. In the video, Titania took off her ring and gave it back to Chad before he crawled into his yellow Jeep and pulled away. "Seems she's been having a long affair with Chad Bradshaw, who decided to break up with her on the same day that her divorce from Bradley Fletcher was finalized."

"Speculation in this double whammy break-up involves the viral picture of Obe and Tati pushed up against a wall in a very seductive position. Tati faced much backlash from fans and critics alike for this picture. However on *The Helen Show*, the pair clarified that it had been a long, stressful night. But it looked to me like the pair were a couple on *The Helen Show*." The anchor laughed as his co anchor chimed in.

"Indeed, Chip," she agreed as she flashed a bright white smile at the camera. "It is unclear where Obe has gone. As the last sightings of him in the California area were right after his appearance on *The Helen Show*. Perhaps the two are going off to meet in private and escape the drama."

The barista set the cup down and slid it across the counter to me. "Here you are, Mr. Obe."

I looked over and into the girl's emerald green eyes. "How much do I owe you?"

She shook her head, and her ponytail flopped from side to side. "Nothing, it's on the house today."

I smiled softly at the girl. "Thank you. Your kindness has been noted." I turned around to leave.

She called out to me as I got to the door. "Mr. Obe?"

I paused and turned around to look at the girl. "Yes?"

"Go after her."

"You had your chance."

"You failed."

"It is too late."

I smiled and nodded my head. "It is much more complicated than you could ever understand." I turned back around and exited the cafe, making my way back to my seat. I reached into my pocket and felt for my wallet and ticket, neither of which was present. I jumped out of my seat and began patting myself down.

"Shit," I spat. "I must have left it at my office." I took off running down the corridor and to my car. The clock on my Ferrari's dash read 3:27 pm and my flight was at 7:00 pm. I had time to get there and back. I would just have to hurry.

I backed out of my spot and started back down the highway. Barreling through the streets, I weaved in and out of traffic. Angry drivers honked their horns and flipped me off. I wanted to get my ticket and get back so I could board the plane on time. Cancun was calling my name. Vacations were always my go-to after saving the world.

After Cancun, I had no idea what I was going to do. I didn't know where I would go. Maybe I would lock myself away in a magically induced coma for a few hundred years while I reflected on my life and choices up to that point. It didn't matter what I did, because it would be without Titania, and she was all I truly needed.

"Leave this place and return to your kingdom."

My kingdom... Perhaps that is what I needed to do. I would go back to my kingdom to rule.

"Alone."

All alone.

“**M**ommy!” Sami came tearing down the stairs and launched herself straight into my arms. “You're home!”

“Hello, my darling!” I greeted, relieved to finally have my little girl back in my arms.

“Mom!” Amira was right behind her little sister, though with less ferocity.

"Hello, sweetheart," I said, pulling her into my hug with Sami. "Oh, I've missed you girls so very much."

"Did you bring us back any presents?" Same old Sami.

"Oh, I'm sorry, darling. I tried to go souvenir shopping, but I just didn't have the time. But I promise you I'll take you girls to Athens and we can all have a wonderful vacation."

"We're just happy to have you home," Amira confirmed, trying to teach her younger sibling to focus on something other than what a person brought her.

"Thank you, dear. Where is Malika?" I asked with hesitation.

"She's in her bedroom," Amira informed me.

"She's sulking," Sami stated bluntly.

"I should go talk to her. Would you two do me a huge favor?"

"Sure!" my girls replied in unison.

"Amira, could you call Chen's and order us some takeout? And Sami, could you go pick out a movie for us all to watch? I think we're long overdue for a family night in."

"That sounds like a great idea, mom," Amira praised.

"Can we have root beer floats, too?" Sami asked.

"Of course! This is the night for it!"

"Yay!" That was all the information that Sami needed to go skidding down to the home theater. Amira pulled out her phone and followed after her as she started ordering from our favorite Chinese restaurant.

With a deep breath, I ascended the stairs to the upper level. What was I supposed to expect? Oberon and I had, of course, seen that once the love sickness caused by the flower was cured, there were no serious lasting side effects and the damage that it had done could easily be repaired. But that didn't stop me from worrying.

I gently knocked on Malika's door. "Who is it?" Her voice was uncharacteristically monotone. There was no joy or confidence the way there used to be.

"It's me. Can I come in?"

"Yeah."

Malika's room was cast in twilight darkness that muddied the white opulence she had decorated and designed within it. The only light in the room came from the glow of Malika's smartphone. Her fashion forward, colorful wardrobe had taken a break, and in its place were gray sweats with the hood pulled up around her head. There wasn't a whisper of makeup on my beautiful daughter's face. And judging by the dark circles under her eyes, she had not had many restful nights since we parted ways not that long ago.

I resisted the urge to turn on the light switch. Malika needed to feel safe at that moment. That meant she called the shots. "Hello, dear."

"Hi, mom," she croaked out. When was the last time she drank any water?

"I feel like you and I need to talk, but I don't want to push you if you're not ready."

"It's okay." Those words and the pulling of her legs up to her chest were the only invitation Malika gave me to sit on her bed.

I sat at the foot, giving her as much space as possible so that she could decide if and when to close the gap. "How are you feeling?"

"Fine."

"Darling." That was the first time I'd taken a motherly tone with her. My children had unfortunately picked up many of my bad habits, including saying that they were fine when they were anything but. I needed her to tell me the truth, and she knew that's exactly what I was asking of her.

A second was all it took to break Malika's reserved cocoon. The tears came hot and fast as she threw herself at me, holding me as tightly as she did when she was a little girl cowering from the thunderstorms. Her embrace was so sudden and severe that her hood tumbled off her head. "I'm so scared, mom." I could barely understand her through her sobs against my stomach. "I don't know what's happening to me."

Oh, no. I'd forgotten about the aftereffects of the damned flower. Everything that happened, from her perspective, would have felt like a dream if she could even remember it. The moment the cure hit her, she would have realized that she lost almost a week's worth of time and not know if anything that transpired in that time was real. It sounded like she didn't talk to anyone in our home, but who knew what she texted to who and what she posted on her various social medias. Those would have been the only clues she had, and they would be just as confusing as the loss of time.

Of course, she was scared.

I gently stroked her braids, trying to soothe her in any way I could. "Talk to me, darling. What's wrong?" I had to act like I didn't understand because I needed to buy myself time to figure out what the hell I was supposed to do.

"I don't remember anything from the last week. I don't remember talking to anyone. I don't remember doing anything. It's all gone."

What was the right thing to do? I didn't know. Not at the moment. It was so much easier to set things right in the earlier centuries. Mortals didn't have anything other than word of mouth and horses to spread word of any strange activities that anyone got up to. There weren't security cameras and NSA agents constantly watching, keeping everything on record. So it would have been easy to simply plant new memories and leave them to their own devices and move on with the lie in their mind.

But 21st century technology would make that impossible. Malika, like most influencers her age, was addicted to her phone. She never went anywhere without it. Rarely skipped a day to post anything. And even if she was on the rare social media cleanse, there were still friends, sponsors, and partners that she kept in constant communication with. There would no doubt be some shred of evidence about what happened during the week that Mab had put Malika under her spell.

Telling her the truth was out of the question. I had put in so much work to make sure my children were never exposed to the truth of their mother's powers, status, and origins. It had caused too many issues in every single relationship I'd tried to have since leaving our kingdom. To tell her what had actually happened would undo all the hard work I'd done to protect Malika and her sisters. And they would never forgive me for the deceit. Well, Sami would probably be forgiving once she knew I was a faerie, but Malika and Amira would never speak to me again.

But it was unfair to my daughter to not give her an answer that would put her mind at ease. She most likely thought she was losing her mind or dying, especially if she had tried to Google her symptoms and had ended up on the less credible side of the internet. I couldn't very well tell her not to worry about forgetting the events of an entire week, especially considering the strange behavior she got up to during that time. No matter how much I would try to assure her there was nothing serious to worry about, she would need proof to truly believe it. And she would feel dismissed and neglected without that proof or any form of concern on my part.

On the other hand, taking her to a psychiatrist or psychologist was dangerous. They would hear her story, force her to go through tests that she didn't need to be subjected to, and ultimately prescribe her some kind of psychotic medication that she didn't actually need. And more than likely it would do more harm than good. To validate her very real and very justified feelings without revealing the truth would mean putting her in more harm's way.

That, of course, didn't mean that she didn't need at least a therapist to speak to about her experience. Something like that could easily lead to PTSD or other worse mental health issues if they had not been dealt with quickly, seriously, and efficiently.

I didn't know what to do. No matter what, nothing would be the same as it was, and something was going to end up broken. Either Malika's psyche, her confidence in my love for her, or my relationship with all of my children. Save for maybe one.

I wish Oberon was there. He would know how to help her. He would know what she needed. He would know what to do. He wouldn't be afraid to tell her the truth.

"What's happening to me, Mom?"

"I don't know," I lied. "But we will figure it out together. And you're going to be alright, my dear. I promise."

As the credits rolled on the movie that Sami had picked out, I looked around to see I was surrounded by sleeping angels and empty takeout boxes. It had taken a long time, but I had finally convinced Malika to come downstairs and join us for dinner and a movie night. I told her that maybe it would take her mind off of things and cheer her up a bit. Throughout the movie, I kept looking over at her to see if I had been correct. I don't know if it had cheered her up completely. But every time I looked, she was in a more comfortable, less closed off position until she was sleeping soundly next to her little sister.

At least she's getting some rest now. That will help.

I quietly and deftly removed myself from the pile of sleeping girls, tucking each one in with the many throw pillows we kept in the home theater. I gathered the empty food cartons and drink cans, turned off the projector and the connecting laptop, and left my three greatest joys sleeping soundly in the darkness. *Guess it's a family slumber party tonight.*

As soon as I closed the door behind me, I sighed with exhaustion and yet my heart rate ramped up. I was so tired, and yet felt restless. I had nothing to focus on. Not caring for my daughters. Not tending to romantic relationships, past and present. Not hurriedly creating some solution to a problem my sister created. And not a conversation with Oberon.

Was I just supposed to sleep after all that had happened? Go to bed and wake up back in my life as if nothing had changed? How could that possibly be? How could it be done?

I needed something to do. Someone to talk to. And there was only one person left that I could possibly talk to about everything that had happened.

My feet took charge on their own, leading me to the garage door. I didn't even register grabbing the keys to my Mercedes until it was time to put them in the ignition.

I pulled out of the garage, closing it behind me as I turned out of the driveway towards the neighborhood entrance. I waved to the evening security guard, who gave me an odd look, but waved me through without stopping me.

The lights of LA wrapped around me, almost guiding me to my final destination; the modern mansion I had dreaded to come to less than a week before.

I turned off the car and the lights, surprised to see no lights on within the home. Or if the lights were on, I couldn't see them from the outside. Oberon would most likely have state-of-the art tinted windows or blackout curtains that would cut his home off from the rest of the world. Still, what guarantee did I have that he was there? Why would I ever think that he would wait for me? Just because he had waited for centuries didn't mean he was going to wait much longer.

A knock on my window scared me out of my thoughts as I screamed. Puck was so scared by my scream of fear that fae jumped as well. "Robin! You really need to stop sneaking up on people."

"Sorry, Catwoman. You'd think you'd be more aware." One of these days, I would understand what fae was saying all the time.

But today was not that day. "Very funny," I said dryly.

"He's not here."

"What?"

"Oberon. He isn't here."

I knew it. "Well, I can wait for him." It was my time to do so anyway.

"Go home, Tati."

"No. It's not the place I need to be right now. I need to talk to Oberon."

Puck rolled faer eyes, shaking faer head. "Fire and gasoline, my Queen."

Yes, we were an explosive combo, prone to self-destructive tendencies that did so much damage. And yet... we kept coming back together. Learning from our mistakes. Improving. This world was so terribly lonely for faeries. We only had each other to look to for comfort and solidarity. And I needed him. "Yes, yes. You think I'd learn from the last six breakups. But I need to see him all the same."

"Looks like you're getting your wish." I followed Puck's gaze to see a car coming over the horizon, the color blocked out by the setting sun. "Please, Tati," Puck pleaded. "Don't hurt him. He won't be able to come back from it again." And with that, Robin Goodfellow disappeared, leaving me to our King.

"You old fool."

"You're going to fail if you go back to your kingdom."

"You're nothing more than an immortal failure."

"Everything you do is full of failure."

"Failure."

"Failure."

"Enough!" I shouted and slammed my fists on the steering wheel as I rounded the curve to see the peak of the mansion that served as both my office and home. I squinted at the car in the distance. Puck wasn't supposed to have anybody over for late night visits. I gave very specific instructions on that. Fae were supposed to be house-sitting, not throwing mad raves like fae used to in the castle halls. I sighed at the thought of coming up on Puck disobeying me.

As I got closer, though, I noticed that the car was a silver Mercedes. The same make and model as… Titania? What in the world could she be doing at my home at that time of night? I let out another, more frustrated sigh as I realized the problem I had been running from turned out to be what I was running back to.

I watched as Puck snapped faer fingers and disappeared in a puff of smoke. Parking the car, opened the door and stepped out. Not looking in her direction yet, I closed the door gently and paused. Finally, I turned to face her. "Hey, you." Was all I could muster.

She let a smile creep across her face as she looked down at her feet and nudged the dirt with the toe of her sandal. "Hello, darling," she replied as she looked back up at me.

I gazed into her eyes, searching for the reason she was there. I wanted to know without having to speak to her. Was it that I had nothing nice to say to her? Or was I simply tongue-tied around her? I wasn't sure, but

I wanted to escape the situation just as quickly as I had arrived.

I took in a deep breath and closed my eyes. Leaning back against my car, I said, "I'll be honest, I didn't think I'd see you so soon."

"Well," she paused and looked deep into my eyes. She was like me; she wanted to know the answer to her question without being asked it. Whatever she was there for, she was nervous of what she was about to do. "I like being unpredictable too sometimes."

I chuckled. It was true; she was always the spontaneous one in our relationship. While I went the 'go big or go home' route, she always went the 'unexpected surprise' route. "I've always loved that about you," I finally confessed to her.

A faint hint of rosy red flushed across Titania's cheeks, indicating her innocent nature of being there. Maybe she hadn't come back to scold me for something. Maybe she had come back for me. For us. "I checked on my girls," she told me as the blush faded from her cheeks.

"How is Malika?" I asked with a quirked eyebrow.

"Malika is... she's no longer lovesick. But the events have left her somewhat traumatized," Titania explained. "I am arranging therapy for all of us, family and individual."

"So," I said as I studied her face. "Everything is fixed?"

Titania smiled softly at me. "Well, there are no immediate emergencies. At least not at my home. Not yet. Is all well with you and yours?"

I grimaced at the thought of being with someone other than her. I didn't have a 'mine' anymore since mine left me over a hundred years ago for a mortal man. "Me and mine? Ha, it's just me, my dear."

Titania shifted uncomfortably from one foot to another, quickly changing the subject at hand. "Is the company still intact? I can't think they did well without you."

"Besides the fire, they didn't mess too much up this time."

Titania looked at me and took in my not-so-convincing tone. "Nothing that can't be fixed?"

"One thing," I admitted as I glanced away from her. One thing wasn't right, but not about the company. The only thing that didn't feel right was being away from my Queen. "But it's irrelevant."

"What is it?" Titania questioned, trying to look into my eyes. I looked back up at her to allow her to meet my gaze. "Do you need help?"

"Nothing, Titania." I looked over at the dark home I had created for myself. Why did I need a home that large when I had penthouses across the city? What was the point of being lonely living in such a large and empty space? I looked back over at her, worry stricken across her face. "What are you doing here? Honestly," I finally had the courage to ask.

She paused, staring at me with hurt and hesitation showing in her eyes. "I... I wanted to see you," she stammered.

I raised both of my eyebrows and brought my head back while I rapidly blinked at her words. "Well, that is a first."

Titania glanced away from me and back to the ground where she had been digging a hole with her toe. "Chad," she started, before pausing. "My fiance and I... we called off the engagement."

I feigned shock, trying to hide the fact that I already knew. "What happened, Titania?"

"Well, the whole experience with Malika left him feeling terribly uncomfortable," she confessed. I understood that and respected the man for doing what he had to do. "And I... Well, I suppose I didn't have the energy nor the desire to make him stay."

"The energy, sure," I said. It had been a long few weeks for Titania and I both, but even more stressful knowing she was coming home to fix her once happy family. "The desire, though?"

"Chad is a very sweet young man. Certainly kind and loving. He was ready to raise the girls as if they were his own..." Titania paused and looked back up at me with a twinkle in her eyes. "But..."

I arched an eyebrow as I glanced at her eyes. "But?"

"He's not my King." I bit my lip. "Oberon, we have broken up and gotten back together more times than we can count in our immortal lives. And yes, when we fight, we hurt each other and the rest of the world terribly. But, we hurt each other and the world more when we're apart." Titania paused as a tear slipped from her eye and trailed down her cheek. "I was wrong, Oberon. And I've been wrong for a very long time."

I was stunned, and my eyes and face showed it. My eyes bulged and my jaw dropped at her revelation. I cocked my head to the side and opened my mouth to speak, but paused as Titania held up her hand.

"I never should have left you or our kingdom," Titania told me for the first time in our immortal lives despite our many breakups. "I am, of course, grateful for my daughters and I don't regret them at all. The only thing I regret was adopting them with someone other than you."

"Titania," I said, pushing myself off the car and taking a step towards her. She was truly the most magnificent being I had ever seen. "I love you."

Those words were all it took for her to release the rest of her tears that she'd been holding back. "And I love you, Oberon."

I ran to her and pulled her into my arms. We spun as I lifted her up into the air and planted a kiss on her delicate lips. She giggled and threw her arms around me. The sun rose behind us and showered us in the morning glory as we found happiness once again.

*K*elsey Anne Lovelady was born in Billings, Montana and grew up in Bozeman until her family moved to Kansas, where she finished high school and went to Johnson County Community College. Her education then took her to the University of Wyoming where she graduated from with a B.F.A. in Musical Theater in 2018.

Kelsey is a late-diagnosed neurodivergent person—she has specifically been diagnosed with Autism and Bipolar Disorder. She is also a proud member of the LGBTQIA+ community. As such, she is always advocating for neurodivergent, disability, and queer representation in media and life.

Kelsey also likes helping others in the indie writing world by offering services such as editing, proofreading, and formatting.

Writing is not the only art form Kelsey dabbles in. She has illustrated children's books, created merch like stickers and t-shirt designs, she runs her own YouTube channel, and she is currently in the process of training to become a drag artist.

She can be reached at: loveladynovels@gmail.com
Kelsey Anne Lovelady on Patreon
Kelsey Anne Lovelady on YouTube
@kelseyannelovelady.bsky.social on BlueSky

Or you can hire her for work as @kelshendrick on Fiverr!

T.B. Wittkofsky is a storyteller, educator, and community builder who uses his personal experiences to help others rise with their stories. With a background in marketing, communications, and mental health advocacy, his work blends strategy with heart. T.B. has taught courses on branding, social media, and entrepreneurship, guiding students and creatives through the evolving digital landscape.

After overcoming challenges like addiction, job loss, and financial instability, T.B. embraced a life on the road in an RV with his wife and three dogs, finding clarity, healing, and inspiration in the journey. He now leads Adventure with Coffee, a blog and podcast that celebrates connection through culture, travel, and, of course, coffee.

As the former president of the North Brunswick Chamber of Commerce and founder of Tea With Coffee Media, T.B. has helped countless entrepreneurs and small businesses find their voice. His advocacy work, including panels on mental health and representation in fiction, underscores his mission to create safe, inclusive spaces for honest storytelling.

Whether mentoring writers, consulting on marketing campaigns, or writing stories that reflect lived truths, T.B. shows up with compassion, curiosity, and an unwavering belief in the power of the narrative.